I0611648

IM PRESS

Golden Dust

Short stories by Igor Shchepetkin

Translated into English
by Anastasia Budnitskaya and Anna Tucker

Edited by Susan Crawford King and Anna Tucker

BOSTON • 2024

IGOR SHCHEPETKIN
Golden Dust. *Short stories*

Translated by Anastasia Budnitskaya and Anna Tucker
Edited by Susan Crawford King and Anna Tucker

ISBN 978-1-960533302
Library of Congress Control Number: 2024938280

Design and illustrations by Lilia Goyzman © 2023–2024

Published by M·GRAPHICS | BOSTON, MA
　　　🖥 www.mgraphics-books.com
　　　✉ mgraphics.books@gmail.com

Printed in the United States of America

Every minute, every chance word and glance, every thought—profound or flippant—the imperceptible beat of the human heart, and, by the same token, the fluff dropping from the poplar, the starlight gleaming in a pool: all are grains of golden dust. Over the years, we writers subconsciously collect millions of these tiny grains and keep them stored away until they form a mold out of which we shape our own particular golden rose—a story, a novel, a poem. From these precious particles a stream of literature is born.

Konstantin Paustovsky, *The Golden Rose*
(translated by Susana Rosenberg)

ACKNOWLEDGEMENTS

Thanks to Olga Blinova (Sergiyev Posad, Russia), Olga Gribanova (Saint Petersburg, Russia), and Yana Yerina (Novorossiysk, Russia) who read the first drafts of these stories in Russian and gave advice and encouragement. A big thank you to Anastasia Budnitskaya (Kaluga, Russia), Susan Crawford King (Bozeman, USA), and Anna Tucker (USA) who offered brilliant suggestions at various stages of English editing.

Thanks to Michael Minayev for stewarding this book into the world. Thanks also to everyone at M•Graphics Publishing.

An additional hearty thanks to my friends Susan Kollin, Robert Ross, and Vladimir Abrosimov for reading the stories in the first edition and commenting on them. I thank my illustrator Lilia Goyzman (Haifa, Israel) for agreeing to work on this project when only one story was written. One look at Lilia's illustrations for the first story, and I wanted to continue writing to see new drawings. Each of her drawings invariably had a creative impulse, without which, perhaps, this book would never have seen the light of day.

Above all, to my children Artem, Alex, and Veronika, my sister Tatyana, and my wife Liliya Kirpotina. She was always there, encouraging my literary endeavors and providing inspiration.

Translator's Notes

Short stories by Igor Shchepetkin absorb your attention with an interesting storyline, and immediately you understand that these are autobiographical sketches. They are even more interesting because of our amusement: Does anyone really face such adventures? Seriously, do they exist in real life?

The style of contemporary prose, along with references to real events and mentioning the places where these events took place, creates a feeling of dialogue with the reader, as if we are all hanging out in one another's company, and the author is telling us his stories, and we laugh, worry, and feel sorrow and surprise through him. The stories are different, same as our life: one inspires us with hope, the other leaves a feeling of sadness in our soul, but each story seems to end with a break, giving a hint that there will be more new stories because life is going on, and it is far from the end.

The main challenge for me, as a translator, was to maintain the author's prose style stripped to the bones and to convey the proper atmosphere of the Soviet times. Some realities then were so unique, that people living in another country may have some difficulties understanding them. However, the dynamics of the narration can be lost behind the long explanations; therefore, I tried to use different stylistic means, not limited to descriptive translation.

It was an amazing experience. Thanks to the author for the trust placed in me.

Anastasia Budnitskaya,
Kaluga, Russia

Illustrator's Notes

I met Igor Shchepetkin on Instagram. He liked my illustrations and drawings, and given his reactions, I felt that he valued freedom and authenticity. When Igor asked me to provide illustrations to one of his stories, *A Walk with a Sketch Map*, I took a risk and proposed a nonstandard layout, where the illustrations would seemingly burst out of the usual rectangular space. Based on how this story made me feel, I choose to use charcoal and ink. To my great joy and delight, Igor completely agreed with my ideas, compositional solutions, and style.

Then, it turned out that Igor had several more stories coming along. This was a very interesting, albeit not easy, process. The stories differed from one another, and I wanted to draw in a similar style for the whole book, based on the style proposed originally for *A Walk*. I had a feeling that Igor completely trusted me, and with this came the desire to "not lose face". I felt a huge sense of responsibility, and I tried to create the most interesting illustrations. In the end, I felt empowered by our mutual understanding, and I fearlessly played with the compositions on the page. Sometimes, the text would "wedge itself" into the illustrations, or conversely, it would freely flow around them, and in other stories, the illustrations would sprawl under or above the text. In addition, I varied the materials, sometimes using only ink, and other times — only charcoal.

The chosen style required that I draw *alla prima*, that is it was practically impossible to make corrections after the fact (at most, I could adjust the proportions of the charcoal drawings in Photoshop and combine several parts into one composition). That is why, perhaps, it sometimes took me several days to consider how to illustrate a section of a story, while the picture composed itself in my mind in its entirety. Only then, I would take some paper and start "copying" from my mind until what I drew matched what I saw in my mind. Usually, I could create appropriate images from my head. Other times, I had to scour the Internet and scientific papers for prototypes to illustrate what the author had in mind. Igor also helped me a lot with references about living in a village as I am very much a city dweller.

Above all, I tried to avoid literal illustrations. When I would run out of ideas, I would dive into the texts and movies that Igor suggested. It helped me a lot that Igor explained the history of how he created his stories, and which movies and books had inspired him. This gave rise to emotional or plot parallels. This collaboration with Igor was incredibly fascinating and rewarding!

I would advise the reader to peruse Igor's stories without haste, thoughtfully, while listening to yourself, your memories, and ideally, for the sake of a stereo effect, while sitting on a porch or in a park, so that you can feel the touch of nature. It seems to me that even hardened city dwellers, like myself, can find moments where they can be in touch with nature, at a summer house, on the sea, or at least at a resort. Believe you me, these memories will blossom anew after reading Igor's stories. They are imbued with incredibly vivid descriptions.

Lilia Goyzman,
Haifa, Israel

Contents

Bear Cape

And you yourself, who are you? You don't know.
You'll find out only later, while stringing the beads of memory.
Once you consist of memories; once you are all a memory.
The most dear, most cruel, and most eternal...[1]

Sasha Sokolov

The river spreads wide. It flows slowly, helping our ship navigate to the north.

I step out of the passenger cabin and am caught by the force of the headwind. I clutch the handrails and feel them trembling from the internal vibrations of the boat. I am overtaken by excitement, and shiver. The handrails are at the level of my chin. I look up: there is the pilot's cabin with huge windows, on the upper deck. In the cabin, a mustached steersman turns the ship's wheel, directing the ship along the fairway, and focusing on the navigational markers. They are barely visible on the distant shore.

I'm standing on the upper deck next to my grandmother. She squints, looking into the distance, spots a fisherman on a sandbar, and smiles. My grandmother has been visiting us for our housewarming party in our new comfortable city apartment. Now we are going to her village.

My dad comes up and invites me to go down to the lowest deck and inspect the engine room. I am happy that I will see the stoker there. I follow my dad down the narrow stairs. It's so loud it's hard to talk. Waving his arms, Dad shouts out some words, points at the parts of the shaking mechanism and tries to explain how it all works. The boat runs on diesel, not coal.

---

[1] A quote from the novel *A School for Fools* by Sasha Sokolov.

So, the stoker is nowhere to be found. At the exit, the senior engineer laughs at me, "We are already flying into outer space, and you are still looking for a stoker."

Disappointed, I return to the upper deck.

It's high water. Endless water reaches almost to the horizon. The navigation season is at its height. Blunt-nosed push-boats stubbornly lead timber-laden barges against the current. Sometimes nimble motorboats cross the Ob River. "We are traveling to Homeland," my grandmother says.

I can't wait to see what this homeland looks like. Having nothing to do, I walk along the corridor beside our cabin and almost collide with two fishermen in rubberized overalls and wading boots. Around the corner, a girl is sitting on a bench, embroidering something on a piece of burlap. She wears a shawl with lilac stripes over her shoulders. A lullaby is heard from the next-door passenger cabin.

Meanwhile, the steamboat is moving forward, occasionally releasing clouds of smoke. Astern, the wake is followed by ribbons of stretching waves, turning them into shimmering ripples.

The next day, the boat lets out a long whistle and moors to the Bear Cape pier. My uncle meets us at the landing, kisses my grandmother, hugs us tightly and takes the suitcases from our hands. But once we come ashore, all subsequent events blend in together and leave no special prints. Such is the nature of a child's memory. Still, I do remember one story that my grandmother often told that year. Parents left their son with their youngest daughter at home alone. The girl was crying, and the boy, trying to calm her down, began to tickle her, and tickled her for so long that she died. The parents came home, and the boy said to them, "Little Tickle lies under the bench." At the end of the story, my grandmother would begin to tickle me, and I would run away.

A few years later, during the school holidays, I came along again with my parents to visit my grandmother. She was very ill, and that summer could be her last.

On one of those days, after a breakfast of crepes and pike caviar, I walked out of my grandmother's house. Chickens were scurrying about in the yard; fishing nets and gunny sacks were drying on the fence. In the shade of the shed, my father was busy with the outboard motor. His greasy hands removed various parts from the inside and laid them out on the bottom of the inverted flat-bottomed boat. Noticing me, he began to name the parts and explained, "Here, I'm going to clean the carburetor." My dad always wanted me to become an engineer. I nodded my head as if I understood. What really attracted me

were the streaks of sticky resin on the rough wood surface of the flat-bottomed boat.

Then my cousin Lyonka came around, showing off his scooter. Its bars and platform were made of pine boards, and there were huge steel bearings instead of wheels on the wooden ax-

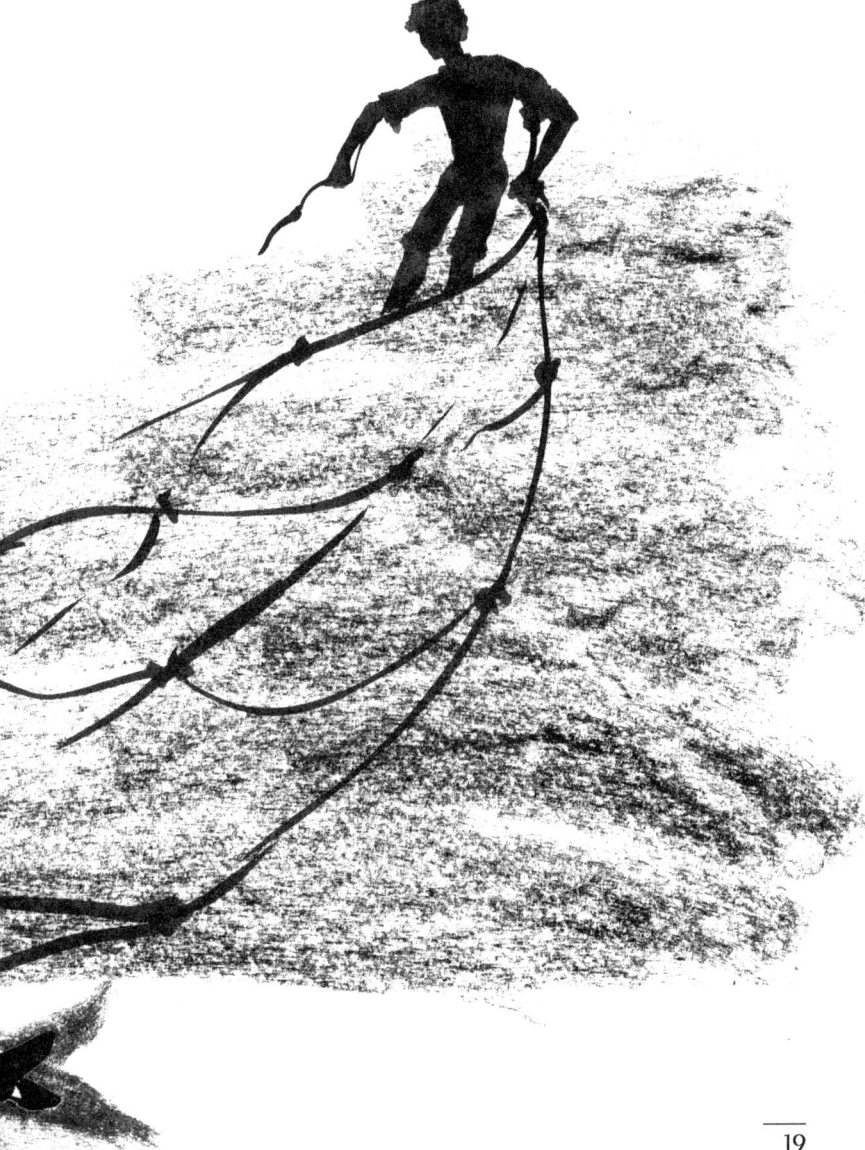

les. Lyonka put this engineering marvel on the path covered with half-logs and pushed off with his left foot. After going a few yards, he pushed off again. He never offered me a ride.

Envious of my cousin's skills, I returned to the house. On the windowsill, next to the scarlet geranium, I found a sketchbook and colored pencils. I put them in my pocket and headed for the pier. I walked along the embankment past the motorboats pulled out of the water. I inhaled a great chestful of river sogginess and took pleasure in the smell of gasoline. Fish scales sparkled here and there underfoot. I stopped just at the water's edge and listened to the pebbles rolling in the oncoming waves.

The rusty carcass of a boat lay between the sand dunes. I sat down at some distance on a huge root, brought here by a spring flood. I took out the sketchbook and began to draw this abandoned boat, overgrown with saltbush. *Long ago, it transported people and cargo*, I thought, and I was so busy with the sketch that I did not immediately notice the girl in a blue bathing suit. She sat by herself under an umbrella, peering into the distance. Her feet were crossed in a way that cast a shadow resembling a mermaid's tail... The pencil in my hand wasn't entirely steady as I drew her into my picture.

By the next morning, the outboard motor was installed on the old flat-bottomed boat. Dad was dressed in overalls and wading boots. Using some clever knot on a short rope, he tied a small dugout boat, called an *oblas*, behind us. We pulled away from the shore and slowly navigated to the other side of the Ob River. The steady chug of the motor blended in with the fog over the sleeping river.

About twenty minutes later, the other shore appeared in the silver haze. Losing the rhythm, the motor rumbled more slowly, snorted, and suddenly stopped. The boat nestled in a sandbar. We dropped anchor and moved a fishing dragnet into the *oblas*. Another hundred yards up to the oxbow lake, we dragged the *oblas* along the wet grass and put it into the water of the oxbow. Deftly paddling, Dad floated off and began to unroll and lower the dragnet into the water. The lead plumbs sank, and the birch-bark floats drifted.

I remained on land to hold the loose end of the net. The sun's rays broke through the occasional clouds, and furious horseflies were swarming in the warmth. They hovered over me and stung. My eyes filled with tears, but I was glad that Dad did not see my distress.

Soon the net was immersed in water. Paddling heavily, Dad made a half round along the dead arm of the oxbow, which was rather wide in this place. Unrolling his wading boots up to the groin, he stepped into the water and, walking along the marshy muddy bottom, dragged the *oblas* out to the cape. The loop of the net narrowed. Suddenly, a commotion started between the floats. We had a hard time pulling the heavy dragnet out of the water and folding it in a spiral on the ground. Dad waded in again and began to untangle the caught fish from the net, throwing them into the sedge grass. The fish wildly swished their tails on the coastal grass and greedily gasped for air with fluttering gills. In excitement, I picked up the squirming bodies and threw them into a gunny sack, which still smelled of the previous catch.

Finally, the job was done. I stripped naked and with breast-stroke crossed the oxbow lake into the thickets of the yellow water lilies, feeling the gentle touch of their long stems.

On the way back, Dad was telling stories about life in the village during the war, "My father was called to the front lines. Soon his death notice arrived... In those harsh years, fish was the food staple. We would grind fish bones into flour and bake cakes from it."

Once, in July, still before dawn, in the same flat-bottomed boat, we went to the mouth of the nearest tributary to hay. The banks of the river, back when it was navigable, were inhabited by the first settlers, called the Ostyak Samoyeds. Later, the river became shallow, people say, due to deforestation. People began to build their houses on the Ob River, a few miles from here. This is how the new settlement appeared. And one could often meet a bear on the country road connecting the new and old areas. Now there were river meadows in the floodplain of the watercourse, a good place for haymaking.

A little later, our relatives rode up in a horse-drawn cart. Patting the sorrel mare on the neck, Mom proudly said, "I harnessed it myself. I only asked for help to tighten the hame strap." My uncle, without speaking, sharpened the blades of the straight-snath scythes with a whetstone and adjusted the handles. He arranged the mowers and showed me how to hold the scythe properly. I joined the line at the very end, behind Lyonka. At first, my scythe kept sticking into the ground. I used a bunch of grass to wipe the blade. After several runs, I began to manage it better and wasn't left behind by Lyonka anymore. During short breaks, I kept asking my aunt about names and healing properties of the mowed herbs.

I leaned on the handle of the scythe and listened. A grasshopper chirped and chirped over the mowing meadow: "tr-r-r-r, tr-r-r-r." There was a dinging in my ears from its chirping.

That's how I spent my summer vacation in this lovely place: fishing, haymaking, going to the pier, or just daydreaming. My grandmother was still in the same condition, neither worse nor better. But after Elijah's Day at the beginning of August, the crisis came. I heard groans from her room. I was scared to look through the half-open door. Not knowing what to do with myself, I took a bicycle from the shed and rode along a potholed, rutted road through the whole village, swerving over and over again around fresh cow dung and puddles full of muddy water. The bicycle's entire frame rattled repeatedly.

The road led to the cemetery, then went down and curved along the creek valley. Leaving the bike on the edge of the swamp, I wandered along the hilly peat bog, picking unripe cloudberries on the way. I lay down at one of the swampy bumps and began to examine it carefully with hope of finding interesting specimens for my herbarium. Today I got lucky; I saw a small, leafy insectivorous sundew plant on one of these bumps, among the gray grass. I carefully squeezed a mosquito on my wrist, put it in the center of the leaf, and observed the leaf's glandular hairs trapping the belly of the insect filled with my blood.

Fascinated by this research, I did not notice a shadow cover the swamp, as if a huge bird flapped its wings. Small splashes fell from the cloud. Forgetting about the new addition to my herbarium, I hurriedly headed for the road. I finally found the bike in the thickets of marsh tea and, leading it by the handlebars, climbed a hillock, from where a panoramic view of the Bear Cape opened. Beyond the village, a wide ribbon of the river flowed in the haze.

Meanwhile, the gloomy cloud near the horizon swallowed up the sun, and rain fell harder.

I returned at dusk, dusty and tired. I put the bicycle in the shed, wiped my face and entered the house. In the hall, a sheet was thrown over a large mirror, and lights were dimmed in the rooms. On the windowsill, next to the geranium, a subdued grave candle flickered. My father stood silently in the doorway to my grandmother's room. Scowling, he curtly asked, "Where have you been?" After a pause, he swayed to the side, and I saw that two neighboring women were washing my grandmother by candlelight. Her pale body was motionless on the bench. One woman held her armpits, another poured water from a ladle.

That night I could not fall asleep for a long time. I was remembering my grandmother's strange tale about Little Tickle. Then I dreamed that someone was tickling me.

Two weeks later, my mother and I were returning home on the Rocket boat in low tide. Dad was staying behind in the village until fall. I looked out of the window, glimpsing islands, steep banks, villages, and squat houses with haylofts. Someone was sitting on a cliff above the river. Halfway into the journey, our boat ran into a tree log and almost tipped over from the strong blow. The log got stuck under one of the hydrofoil's splash boards. Mom took a nitroglycerin pill out of her purse and put it under her tongue. The navigator and the captain armed themselves with hooks and struggled to release the log from the hydrofoil. A mechanic in a diving suit dived and looked for damage. There was none. Little by little we reached the town.

School started in September. In the Literature class, I received a homework assignment to write an essay called "How I Spent My Summer Vacation". I plodded dejectedly home from school. The wind whirled yellow leaves at me. At home, I locked myself in my room. I sat all evening over a draft notebook but did not write a single line. That night I had a fever. I was ill for a long time, and when I recovered, the teacher did not ask me for this assignment. But the events of those years have continued to disturb me, and the unwritten essay remains in my memory.

I look into the past as if into a mirror from which the cover has been pulled off. And twenty years later, I am writing the essay I couldn't write before.

I have a narrow strip of paper in front of me. I twist it and glue the ends together, making a Möbius loop. Then I lean back in the creaking chair, rub my forehead and glance at the corner of the neighboring house. The room is stuffy. Breaking my fingernail on the latch, I open the door to the balcony, cross the threshold, and seize the painted wood of the rails. In the corner, on a small table, a grasshopper sits in a large glass jar covered with gauze, and chirps loudly. Its knee appears huge under the magnifying glass of the jar's curvature. I carefully lift the edge of the gauze and throw in a tiny morsel of food. The chirping of the grasshopper reverberates off the walls of the neighboring houses. And, like a fragment of a dream, a blade of grass flies into the room with a gust of wind.

ON OLD ACHINSKAYA STREET

I learned the alphabet and can read haltingly, while you already know the code of another world. Last summer, I found myself in this world during a storm. Awash in salty sweat, I reached the shore after a shipwreck. The agony of my ancestors remained in my memory. The pain subsided. Starting from the wrecked ship, I decided to measure the length of the coast and ended up in the world of fractals. I walked through the thickets and broke off a branch. The stump started bleeding. It was murder. My surroundings abruptly changed, and I saw women and their wild dances. Later, I felt the warmth of your hands. I embraced your body, enjoying the dance, and thought about love. Is it mysticism or a magical veil, dense and opaque in one place and completely transparent in another? The repeatedly reflected fire of the sun illuminates the road. I walk, inhaling the ephemeral fragrances.

Where to begin? It doesn't matter really—in a garden, in a vegetable patch, in a gully; in the ravine of the Milan fortress; by a water pump in the winter, covered in frozen streaks (I don't remember the ice patches around it to ever be sanded) at the intersection of Old Achinskaya Street and School Lane. I should add that once, when some neighborhood kids were pumping water, some unlucky fish splashed out of its elephant trunk spout right into the bucket; obviously, the water was supplied straight from the river.

My grandfather picks up two buckets of ice-cold water and carries them on a creaking shoulder yoke. The trip is long; and afterwards Grandfather also climbs the stairs to the second floor of the wooden apartment building. There, in the unheated outer hallway of our dwelling, sits a barrel for drinking water. Here we keep firewood in the winter, next to a bucket of sauerkraut and a half-empty forged chest that reeks of ancient naphthalene. In the inner hallway that doubles as a kitchen, there is a washstand with a bucket for waste water under it. A woodstove occupies the center of the kitchen. There is a table, a bed, and a handmade bench on one side of the room. The bench can be used for sleeping. There is the Portrait of an Unknown Woman by Ivan Kramskoy above the kitchen table.

The woodstove and an open doorway separate the kitchen from the bedroom, the only other room. There is a bed right

behind the stove; a wardrobe and a daybed are arranged along the adjacent wall. There are two windows with a chest of drawers between them on the opposite side. The right window is bricked up, plastered, and whitewashed. A carved wardrobe towers to the left of the entrance to the room. A table stands in the center of the room. There is a large icon hanging in the corner. In this very apartment, with Grandma Fenya and Grandpa Ivan, I shall spend my childhood—from the moment I was brought in a small zinc tub from the neighboring town where I was born until I am seven (I would never go to preschool), and I finally move into my parents' apartment in a newer neighborhood.

There is quite a steep one-flight staircase, with worm-eaten wood railings, that leads to the second floor of the building where our apartment is located. How many steps does it have? There is no exact answer to this question although I already know how to count. I think it has at least thirteen. Using a shovel and a hatchet, my grandfather carefully clears the steps of snow and ice so that it would be easier to climb them while carrying firewood or water buckets. Warm mittens, made of scratchy sheep wool, are on his hands. Before climbing the stairs, he removes the buckets from the yoke and then carries them in his hands; otherwise, the front bucket would knock against the steps.

There is a small landing at the top. There is one more door to the right of ours, to another apartment. Its owners left for good, so the door has been boarded up. Their stove must have been destroyed with a crowbar; the same will happen to our stove when our turn to leave this place comes. Therefore, our closest neighboring space behind the wall is a frozen and unexplored expanse where it might be difficult to breathe. It is a nice place for ghosts. Clotheslines are stretched on the same landing. There is a trapdoor to the attic above the clotheslines, and even higher, a dark dormer window in the shape of an inverted heart. It faces the small yard laid with sandstones and another building, where the Katkovs and the Okamovs live.

Our neighbors can see our signals posted on the washing lines: a white sheet signifies the betrayal of tin soldiers; a skirt informs of the lack of milk, men's trousers proclaim the lack of eggs. When we need Dr. Kurkina, we set my potty on the wide railing of the open staircase. The Katkovs own the only telephone in our entire street; the number is 50–15. They are the ones who call places and ask for people and things we need.

I like to blow soap bubbles and launch paper doves from the top of the stairs. The best of those reach the center of the yard. In the summer, hop plants grow thickly among the wooden pillars that support the stairs. Under the flight of stairs, there are entrances to the apartments of our downstairs neighbors, the Bulantsevs and the Vyugovs.

Our building at 11 Old Achinskaya Street, and our entire yard, or rather, its remains, were demolished a long time ago. But they still stand in my imagination and, perhaps, in the minds of other people who lived here; if they are still able to remember anything, of course. A residence is a living creature with its own soul. Where does this soul settle when the structure passes away? Sometimes I dream that I am standing in front of a tall gate to our yard, but the gate is firmly locked. There is no access anywhere, and I do not know how to enter this serenity of warmth and glow and hear the conversations of my childhood. Shall I try to write a verse that will open the way?

> *To break the iron lines' array,*
> *To leave behind your sweetheart's face;*
> *To walk an old abandoned way*
> *Where poplar branches interlace.*
> *To let the rainbow bubbles fly*
> *And hover under the tall stairs.*

To watch wolf spiders carry mail,
And knock, and wait for the reply.
To see the paper flock at play
Inside the willows' sunny weave
And send a matchbox raft away
To boldly go, to sail, to live.

As I say the last word, the gate opens, smooth and silent...

In March, the snow starts melting. Snowmelt from the street leaks under the locked gates and flows across the entire yard. My grandfather or one of our neighbors digs a long shallow ditch for the stream: all the way to the gully. It is fun to send a splinter floating from the gate and follow it along the entire path of the stream. I sometimes help this little vessel along if it gets stuck somewhere.

Gradually, thawed patch after thawed patch, the yard is clear of the snow. Tanya Okamova, a girl next door, picks the first dandelion and coltsfoot flowers and makes a wreath. I take it in my hands, and the yellow fringe of flowers slowly wilts.

Once I went with Grandfather to White Lake for kerosene. There was a kiosk the color of dried blood that looked like a garage, on the endless shore. It sold hardware; a shoe shiner hunched next to the kiosk on a small bench with a set of multi-colored shoe polish. I did not know why Grandfather wanted to buy kerosene since we had electricity. Apparently, he was afraid of being caught without light, so he kept a kerosene lamp. I remember Grandfather using it once when power went out at home.

Light bulbs in our house burn out often. When my dad comes back, he is always asked to change a light bulb or fix the electric hot plate. He works in a factory, and he can twist a spiral from nichrome wire for this hot plate and place asbestos where necessary for insulation. I'm terribly interested and watch him make repairs. When a new bulb lights up, my grandparents are in absolute awe. They really are! Back in the day, they had to burn long dry wood splinters for illumination. If you look at the historical photo "Ilyich's Light Bulb", you will see a scene which is very similar to the one seen in our apartment from time to time.

After every meal, my grandparents pinch their fingers together and make the sign of the cross in front of the icon that hangs in the corner just under the ceiling. It shows a barefoot old man with a beard. He holds a globe in his left hand and points severely with the fingers of his right hand, as if he is admonishing me for skipping Geography homework. I have nothing to worry about: my Geography still fits into the boundaries of the yard and a couple of nearby streets. I once asked my grandparents who God is and where he lives. I was told that it was a *sin* to speak like that. That is a new word for me. Now, I would say that I had no sin to hide...

It is getting dark, and Grandfather brings firewood from the entry room, stacks the logs in a stepped pyramid in the woodstove, opens the blower and kindles a new fire. Then he lights a cigarette from a brightly flaring splinter and greedily absorbs the smoke into his lungs. Sitting on a small handmade bench, he smokes his roll-your-own cigarette until the cigarette butt burns his fingers.

Leaning against the doorframe, I sit on the kitchen bench and stare blankly at the living flame in the firebox. Finally, we go to bed. One large light bulb, as bright as a hundred candles, hangs from the ceiling beam on a curved wire under an orange muslin lampshade, already fairly faded. My grandfather, in blue long johns and a worn-out flannel shirt, reaches for the switch and says, "Well, shut ya peepers!" I slide under the covers into the smell of clean linen, and the light goes out. I can still hear the blessing of the crackling logs for a while. Then everything sleeps.

In winter, the house is cold in the mornings. Here, someone opens the door to the entry room, and a light icy cloud floats inside. I lie in bed under a quilted comforter, waiting for my grandfather to rekindle the stove and for the room to warm up.

My home on Achinskaya street still lives in my feverish mind:
Here, Grandfather carries a bundle of sacrificial wood upstairs
While Grandson plays cards with grandmother Lina.
Grandfather enters and latches the door, starts a fire in the stove.
We brew tea and drink it with raspberries.

My grandfather often goes out to the country to hunt. Before the war, he was a professional hunter and delivered furs to the government officials. But I don't know that yet, because I can't even understand what a government is. He brings home wood grouse, hare and other game. My grandfather makes snares from the same nichrome wire to catch hares in the forest. The hare gets trapped and freezes to death.

One day Grandpa brought a frozen hare and placed it under the Christmas tree. The hare lay there in all its beauty (next to a toy Father Frost) until it thawed. Then it disappeared — a Christmas miracle. Another time, Grandpa bagged an unfrozen hare and hung it by its front paws in the kitchen to clean. This activity distracted my grandmother from her housework, and she ran outside in disgust. I stayed; I was very curious. My grandfather pulled out the innards and threw some into a bucket, others into a large bowl. Thick drops of blood fell from the hare's ribs into a basin, like pomegranate seeds.

After eating the hare, we do not throw away the hollow bones. Grandpa makes them into hunting calls for hazel grouse. He skillfully cuts a triangular hole in the bone, using a rasp-file, and inserts a piece of wax in there. When hunting, my grandfather blows into a call; hazel grouse flock to him from all over the forest, and he kills them. The enticing power of the hare keeps working until the hunting call is lost in thick grass.

Stiff stubble slowly grows on grandpa's face, and I love to touch it. He shaves it off every two weeks. This is an entire ritual that I have learned well. First, my grandfather takes some green paste and spreads it on a wide leather belt. Then he pulls out a razor blade from a cardboard sheath (he hides the razors on top of the chiffonier so I can't get to them) and runs it flat along the tightly stretched belt for a long time, every now and then checking the blade for sharpness. When the razor is sharp, he cuts thin chips from a chunk of laundry soap with a kitchen knife into an old metal cup (he has likely been using this cup since WWII); then he adds water, whisks a thick foam with his shaving brush and covers his face with the foam. Finally, looking askew into an irregularly-shaped shard of a mirror and deftly wielding the blade, Grandfather shaves off his stubble, and blood shows here and there through the remaining foam. After shaving, he covers the cuts with pieces of newspaper and paces around the room like that, grinning slyly and emanating the invigorating scent of Triple Eau de Cologne.

Our yard is separated from the street by tall wooden gates with a smaller man door in them. A huge iron ring hangs from the man door at my shoulder level. To enter, I have to grab this cold ring with both hands and, turning it, push the man door with all my strength. The big gates are closed at all times. They are only opened when firewood is delivered for the winter. Once I participated in chopping firewood; I didn't chop anything myself, of course: I was still too young for this, but, standing in a clearing, I broke branches off the birches to make whisks for the bath-house. The firewood shed is at the bottom of a steep slope, and the truck cannot drive up to it, so the firewood is unloaded in the upper part of the yard, near the cellar that smells of creosote (this smell reminds me of the railway tracks nearby). Later, Grandpa and my dad split birch chocks into logs and take them to the shed and the entry room for storage, until winter.

The shed sits straight across from the door of the Okamovs' apartment. By summer, the last woodpile in the shed disappears, and we can play inside and even throw a small knife at the walls. It smells pleasantly of old sawdust and birch bark. On a sunny day, the inside of the shed glows with beams of light that come streaming in through the cracks like fragile flickering feathers. It feels like heaven. There is a black box with a gramophone and 78 rpm records stored in the shed. To get the gramophone going, one needs to turn its handle several times, and then the disc with the recording begins to rotate.

One summer day, I was sorting through all the rubbish in the shade and got fascinated by a record with the coat of arms of the United Nations. Unfortunately, the reproducing needle was broken. Tanya Okamova was a girl from next door, and we asked her parents to get a new needle, but they never did. Perhaps, they were not interested in listening to old records, or

they may have been believers in delayed gratification. Anyway, we have played and continue to play records; we spin and spin them, and the gramophone sounds good enough to us.

> *In a dusty shed there sits a gramophone.*
> *Turn the handle, and it will grumble: "UN-oooo".*

There are gray gravestones paving the slope of our yard; they are made of sandstone, with carved lines of strange characters and words. There are only five gravestones, and they create two steps. We think that these gravestones were put there by someone to prevent erosion. I do not know how they happened to be in our yard and where they were taken after the buildings were demolished; and no one can tell anymore. I can read a little, but the letters on the gravestones are different from those in my books. Possibly, this is the Early Cyrillic alphabet.

I often play here with Tanya Okamova. Saltbush grows through one split between the gravestones.

I will continue to string the beads of memory and, perhaps, I will discover some new things about myself, sorting them out like prayer beads that rattle in my soul.

Here, I have a children's butterfly net in my hands, and I run with it around the yard, hunting cabbage butterflies, mourning-cloak butterflies and brimstone butterflies. It probably sounds arrogant, but I caught my first butterfly at the age of six, just like Vladimir Nabokov.

There, I am holding a red plastic Vostok rocket, similar to the one in which Gagarin flew into space a year before I was born. If I pump water into it, it launches pretty high above our yard, throwing a foamy jet from its nozzle with a hiss, like one coming from the neck of a Soviet Champagne bottle. Ivan Katkov, my neighbor, leans on the railing of his own porch, located above the Okamovs' apartment, and observes my game. Perhaps he is afraid that the rocket will land on his unprotected head or hit one of the windows of his dwelling. He says something to my parents, and after that they don't let me run my tests any more.

My memory is selective, but it does not work like a voting box. Nobody requires me to memorize my childhood while I live in this moment, so I remember only what is interesting, and necessary, to myself. For example, I remember the fact that Ghena Bulantsev lives on the first floor, and he is a very tall guy. People say he does not fit in his bed and puts a stool nearby for his feet or head at night: it depends on which direction he lies down on the bed. Still, this is enough; this is something my memory can hold on to. Grandma Varya, Ivan Katkov's wife, is missing a finger on her hand; her finger was severed at the weaving factory. I don't remember anything else about her. It seems that she sat on a bench on her high porch all those years.

There are also various interesting (both useful and not) items, and I could play hide and seek and remember where they are, especially if they have a time stamp on them. You may ask where on earth the pliers are. I will answer that it is very simple. This rust-spotted tool rests in the bottom drawer of the carved cabinet in our living room. There are tons of nails of different sizes in the same drawer; they are so bent that you will never find two identical ones. The hardest thing to find in our yard is a bicycle. Indeed, you will find neither a new bicycle, nor a rusty one. There is only a dream of it.

Below our yard, there is a large gully, where the surrounding community from our odd side of the street dumps their garbage and drains sewage from garbage buckets. This makes our yard even more inaccessible, resembling an old fortress. However, it's not sedge that grows at the bottom of this moat. Some resourceful neighbors grow potatoes there. So, no one is surprised why the smell of sweat is so obvious here at harvest time. A creek runs at the bottom of the gully and somewhere beyond joins the clear river Lethe (or maybe it has a different name). A lonely poplar grows from the gully. My grandfather once said that he planted a poplar branch many years ago, and it grew into this wonderful tree. It's still hard for me to believe.

If I stand on the edge of the gully and loudly shout "Echo!", then it will resound. I can't think of another word to shout like that in one breath.

For Tanya Okamova and I, the gully is a source of various small bottles and penicillin flasks for our pretend pharmacy. There are also rumors that one of our neighbors once found a crushed human skull in the gully. I secretly dream about discovering some real bones under a layer of clay. Tanya and I collect multicolored shattered glass and pieces of glazed ceramic in the gully for our treasure-making game. This is one of our most exciting activities. We dig a hole, put precious fragments into it and cover it all with a big piece of glass, and then observe our treasures from the Hellenic era through it. Afterwards, we cover the treasure with soil. In the end, the most difficult thing is to keep the place where it is buried a secret.

I dig a hole behind a gravestone
And settle my favorite rock in it
Surrounded by colorful shards
Of kaleidoscopic glass.
I cover it with sticks and bark
And will never tell where it's hidden.

To the west of our yard, there is another yard across the street near the gully; I have not explored it yet. Its gates on the street side are always closed. It is difficult to reach it by walking the edge of the gully because the slope is too steep. Sometimes I see a girl dreaming of wildflowers, at the edge. Perhaps she, too, is looking for bits and pieces for her own treasure-making game. But one day a disaster strikes. The girl died. People said she ate some berries and died from acute appendicitis. She might have eaten unwashed gooseberries, or even dogberry, or nightshade.

Nightshade grows in abundance on the edge of the gully, and its berries look attractive due to their perfect shape. People put out many wreaths and painted-tin flowers in the street as a memorial. I had never gotten to know this girl, and didn't know her name. Of course, I could ask my neighbors later what her name was, or make up a name for her. But where are these neighbors now, especially since the street does not exist anymore (and we agreed that I would not fabulate anything that did not happen).

If we walk up the street from our house towards the community water pump, we can see there an apartment building[2] on our side, where Yura Kubantsev lives with his parents and grandmother. I rarely see his parents. Like mine, they usually work long hours. Their yard also faces the gulch, and this unites us. Yura is a little older than me; I cannot say that we are very friendly. We get bored of each other's company. Yura can sing and play the accordion, not the mandolin, whose sound and shape I relate to (I dream, my dear reader, of floating down the Lethe River one day, using a mandolin-shaped paddle). But these days I sometimes visit Yura, and his grandmother usually asks me to listen to his progress in playing music. Stretching the bellows of the accordion — they resemble the map of the USSR — Yura sings, articulating each word, "Do Russians want war? Just ask every mother's mind, at least just ask a soldier's wife, whether the Russians, whether the Russians want war..."

I listen attentively and imagine my grandfather Andronit, my father's father, fighting in tank-supported infantry. During

---

[2] Thirty years before the events described herein, Nikolai A. Klyuev, a notable Russian poet and former political prisoner, lived in this building. He was seriously ill. He wrote to his friends that he was able to see the summer only from the miserable yard, when he was dragged out to sit by a pile of firewood in the evenings: "I haven't been to the bath-house in a long time, it's far from my dwelling and the path goes through gullies; I can't get there... It's already fall here; it's cold, there is mud up to the horse-collar; some boys are shouting behind a wooden fence, and a red-haired wench curses them out; a nauseating stench rises from the horrible common wastewater basin under the washstand..." (1936).

an attack, he was running with other infantrymen, following the tanks, and fell somewhere far away in the endless valley of that star war; he was not protected by any armor... The tanks keep going, leaving deep hot furrows in the dusty desert. Gradually, the scarlet dust dissipates like mist, and the Little Prince could be seen standing in this distant region of an alien planet.

A few years later, Yura's family will move to the same subdivision where I will live with my parents. He will have a lot of tin soldiers, and sometimes we will play together.

Now is a good time to return to the people who share my yard. The Okamov family has two daughters: Mila and Tanya, the younger. Sometimes Nina, Mila's friend, shows up. She is the most beautiful of them, and I get a feeling that she is their sister too. Anyway, I never talk to her. Tanya is only two years older than me. She has almond-shaped black eyes and chiseled cheekbones. I would like to say that she and I are friends, but I think it would be more appropriate to say that she's my playmate, and that she allows me to be her playmate. We have pretend games of house, pharmacy, and grocery store on the gravestones because they lie flat. Tanya has real scales, and we weigh different pretend wares on them. For example, pieces of rotten wood represent smoked fish. We put balance weights in the opposite scale pan. Tanya's mother works in a store, so she lets us borrow weights for our games.

It is getting dark. Tanya draws a hopscotch grid on the ground with a sharp stick, and we play, throwing a piece of bottle glass into numbered squares. She always wins, but I still enjoy playing with her again and again.

I can no longer avoid all the doubts in the intricacy of my mind.
I just close my eyes to the struggle, being silent and blind.
Under the cover of night and light, I stand in the wind for a time
Repeating my childhood testaments, like this counting rhyme:
"On the Golden Porch sat
    the King,
        the lady's maid,
            the prince,

the princess,
the shoemaker,
the tailor..."

I love visiting the Okamovs. Past the threshold, there are steps going down. The sun almost never penetrates into the kitchen, as it is a semi-basement. The Okamovs often heat the house with coal. They grow tomatoes in the summer and in the autumn put the still-unripe fruit into chests of drawers, between window frames, and probably in some other odd places. The back room, where I am not allowed, is filled in by my imagination, and sometimes in my sleep I walk the space at dusk. The windows with lace curtains face the gully, with heavy chairs close to them, twilight permanent in the room. Then I levitate over the gully and return back to the room.

The Okamovs have a male cat (or maybe it's a female). Tanya likes to look for eye-boogers in the eyes of the creature. Once she finds some, she carefully cleans them off with something. Also, Tanya told me that she loves horses. I should also mention that she was the one to introduce me to ladybugs. In August, branches of chokecherry in our yard are covered with spider webs, and under the spiderwebs, many insects swarm. These are aphids; they are enemies of leaves. It turns out that ladybugs eat aphids and do good. I also want to be useful by killing those who do harm. Specifically, cabbage butterflies lay eggs that turn into cabbage-eating caterpillars. Tanya and I catch cabbage butterflies and tear off their wings.

Once, when Mila, Tanya's older sister, was visiting my place, I asked her to lie in my bed. She undressed, leaving on just a pink full slip and lay down under the covers next to me. A strange yet inviting aroma came from her. There was a tapestry depicting The Three Bogatyrs[3] by Victor Vasnetsov above the bed. Vigilantly, Ilya Muromets peered from under a patterned gauntlet

---

[3] *Bogatyrs* are characters of medieval East Slavic legends. Tradition describes bogatyrs as warriors of immense strength, courage, and bravery.

into the steppes in the distance. I felt my mother loom over us, saying, "Okay, that's enough playing silly games."

At the edge of the gully, as if at the end of the world, a wooden outhouse sits alone. Neither of the two buildings in our yard have indoor plumbing, and that's why the outhouse was built on the cliff. A path leads to the latrine; it has been trodden since time immemorial, and it will be for ever after (or so it seems to me). Once every summer, a woman in a duster visits the neighborhood along the gully and sprinkles bleach powder into the latrine and on the slope where the residents dump sewage from garbage pails.

My mother fears that I might fall into the latrine and drown, so I almost never go there; my potty is under my bed. In winter, stalagmites of frozen feces grow around the latrine hole. Ivan Katkov, our neighbor, whom we nicknamed "Katok" behind his back, gloomily and dedicatedly breaks off these growths with a bayonet shovel. Tanya Okamova stands behind Katok

and makes cranking movements with her hand at the level of his lower back, as if starting a car. Why does Tanya not have the slightest respect for him? We have yet to study this phenomenon or ask Viktor Erofeev, an expert on the Russian soul.[4]

My mother tells me that Katok often babysat me when my grandmother went shopping. I don't remember it; I must have been too young. The years my tale takes place in lasted so long that Katok had time to live and to die. When Katok passed, my

---

[4] An allusion to the novel *Encyclopaedia of the Russian Soul* (1999) by Victor V. Erofeev, a Russian writer and literary critic.

grandfather burst into a dance, "I've outlived Katok, I've out-lived Katok!" He was truly happy, and I didn't know why...

Hemp plant grows thickly behind the Okamovs' house, right at the path down into the gully. Here, I can look into their windows if I climb onto stone skirting filled with slag from their stove. I want to check if there is a large wall-mounted cuckoo clock in the room although the windows are still curtained off. The hemp reaches to my shoulders. In late summer, Tanya and I break the stems off at the root (they crunch) and build a hut; it is our pretend home. The smell of the withering hemp still reminds me of my childhood. I wish I could spend a night in this hut, with a small flashlight, attracting astonished night butterflies, and, looking into the darkness of the night, stare at the stars and cry from happiness and anticipation, remembering my childhood.

> I will light a lamp dimly in that tall-grass hut at night,
> To attract a flock of moths from the gully, summoned by the light.
> And at dawn in that gully, scything high,
> The croppers walk freely, that sedge cutting by.
> When the ashes of silver dew fall through the spider web,
> They will revive the stream and stop the motion of the scythe.

Outside the gates of our yard, such a huge poplar grows that I can't wrap my arms around it. A bench hides under the tree. My grandparents often sit here on summer evenings and watch the pattering passers-by. The street is unpaved and not even graveled. I like to play under the whispering poplar. I pick a leaf from the tree, put it on the back of my hand and hit it hard with the palm of my other hand: the leaf rips with a bang.

A pretty deep ditch cuts across the road and makes it impossible for cars to pass through. That's why the street is so quiet. This ditch must have once been connected to the gully, and I can almost hear the rattling of a rusty chain of the drawbridge. A wooden pedestrian bridge with a railing spans the ditch to the Berezina bath-house. The boards of the bridge bounce when people cross. Nasty looking nails that remind me of the

Spanish Inquisition stick up from the boards here and there; you have to be very careful not to hurt your feet. It is also dangerous to hold on to the railing: you can easily get a splinter. Some passers-by, afraid to trip and fall, cross the ditch through runny mud that makes squelching noises under their feet.

I sit under the poplar tree and think my own thoughts. People walk by. Some guy comes into the people's yards and asks if anyone wants to get their knives and scissors sharpened. A glazier offers to glaze the windows. I would like both the glazier and the knife-sharpener to come over and do something useful. But my grandfather explains with pride that everything of ours is sharp and the windows are just fine. Maybe both the glazier and the knife-sharpener still wander through this territory of human memories and unfulfilled hopes; professional habits die hard.

At the corner of our Old Achinskaya and Oktyabrskaya streets, the Berezina bath-house nestles in a hollow. The men's days and the women's days alternate. Even trains sometimes collide, when the tracks are not a loop and the schedule is disrupted, the rails are rusted, or maybe the switchman messed something up; but it has never happened so that everyone washed on the same day. Therefore, some evenings, let's call them even days, sitting on a bench in front of the gates of our yard, you can see only women with flushed faces and towels on their heads in place of white kerchiefs wandering sluggishly from the bath-house. On other days, the odd ones, only men will walk along the street with birch sauna whisks under their arms and toiletry bags filled with stuff. I have also been to this bath-house, and more than once. But one day... Should I tell you this one or not? Hmmm, this is what happened: I was there on a women's day. I remember a naked woman with large breasts standing in front of me and holding a tin basin full of water and a washcloth. My memory hides other women from me: that day I fell on the slippery tile floor and almost blacked out.

Eventually, my hair grows out, and they take me to a barber next door to the bath-house. I don't like getting my hair cut there because one of the barbers has a long beard, and I really don't want him to cut my hair. I'm afraid of him. I watched him shave a man with a straight razor and saw drops of blood appear on the client's cheek.

From the intersection where the Berezina bath-house is located, Oktyabrskaya Street winds downhill to the church (the street does not end there, unlike some modern novels). On the eve of St. Nicholas Summer Day, I walk with my grandparents through the churchyard. A beggar woman in a tightly tied dark scarf stands at the gate. She is hunched over so that her face is

not visible, and holds her hands together, palms up, clenched in the shape of a boat, and whispers. Her hands shake. I am filled with curiosity and want to know what she is saying. We walk into the church; there is a smell of wax candles; people make the sign of the cross with pinched fingers; but even this does not help me to look inside myself. I keep looking at the world, wide-eyed, and ask questions, tugging on my grandmother's hand.

One day, a motorbike circus came to our street. They set up a colossal barrel near the bridge over the ditch; that part of the street was impassable to cars already anyway. Spectators with tickets climbed a steep staircase to a high balcony at the top edge of this "adrenaline-filled" barrel. It was packed. I sneak up

and, standing on tiptoes, look in fascination over the edge of the barrel at the fearless blindfolded motorcyclists who race at great speed along the inner vertical plane of this cylindrical abyss.

Our house is a ten minutes' walk from the White Lake. You can wander along the paths trampled down by thousands of feet, walk along them round and round, as if along the edge of a gigantic black hole that attracts all living things and even light. Long ago, there was a fountain here, and a monument to Stalin stood on the shore. Now the water in the lake is dark and heavy, and water striders glide on its surface. Lonely anglers catch the last remaining fish for their cats. Flocks of sparrows sit in the branches of the weeping willows growing along the shore, and magpies hop on the paths and peck at cigarette butts and sunflower seed hulls.

People often swim in the lake during the day and in the evening. Sometimes they drown. Once, a woman screamed heart-rendingly on the shore for her drowned child. That was not the only case. Every year something similar happens on the lake, and someone shouts in our yard, "The divers are here!" All of us run to watch as they dive deep into the water, looking for the drowned.

In those years, a wooden movie theater loomed on the lake shore. *Fantômas* was shown there, and I thought it was a really scary movie. I covered my face with my hands and squinted through my fingers as Louis de Funès shouted, horrified: "Help! There is a hanged man in my room! Help!"

Later, the movie theater will be demolished, and a stone spaceman will be erected in its place to make time flow backwards. Indeed, a black swan glides on the blue surface of the

water like a ghost; it sees its reflection and the sky full of secrets. I think this is the same bird, a black swan I once saw on
a taiga lake. The Lethe River flows in and out of the lake. The
river will never run dry.

> *A fast current creates an ice-hole*
> *where you can get some water of life,*
> *and carefully carry it to your distant dwelling*
> *on a creaking yoke under the protection*
> *of the silent moon and, to your satisfaction,*
> *without any ulterior motive, knowing*
> *that there will be aspiration and vexation,*
> *tension and inspiration,*
> *birth and salvation.*

I often get specks in my eyes. If my mother is home when
this happens, she spits on a rolled-up corner of a handkerchief
and removes the speck of dust or a blade of grass. Once a speck
(or maybe it was a blade of grass) landed in my eye when my
mother was at work, and Grandma Fenya did not know how to
help me. She took me to the telegraph station in the town center, where my mother worked as an economist. We went by bus,
and I cried the whole way. A gypsy woman handed me a piece
of candy, and I immediately put it in my mouth. Grandma was
afraid that I might get jinxed, and she ordered me to spit the
candy out, which I did immediately.

After a long, long ride, we finally arrived at our destination
and walked under a stone arch into the courtyard and to my
mother's place of work. I found myself in the center of a room,
where bespectacled ladies were sitting at desks. Mom came
up to me and said, "Let me see". Then she spit on a rolled-
up corner of her handkerchief and pulled this "log" out of my
eye. Gherasim Dmitrievich entered the room and grinned. At
the telegraph office, he was the boss of carrier pigeons at that
time. I asked, "Where is the telegraph here?"

My grandfather works as a loader at the Regional Community of Consumer Cooperatives (if our town were a female

breast, this place would be located just on its nipple). When it's time for him to come home, my grandmother sits by the only window facing the street and waits. It's getting dark outside, and I sit next to my grandma near the windowsill. "Here comes Grandfather", Grandma Fenya jumps up from her chair as she spots the drunken Grandpa staggering down the hill to the gate. Soon, I can hear him walking heavily up the stairs. Finally, Grandpa crosses the threshold of our dwelling, and Grandma quickly pushes our little bench towards him. After sitting down, my grandfather takes off his worn-out kirza nailed boots. Then he patiently unwinds dirty foot cloths from his sweaty feet (I never wore such). His feet can finally breathe. Grandma Fenya says quietly, "Va-a-nya!" In response, Grandpa bleats like a ram, makes a face, and sticks his tongue out.

On long winter evenings, my grandmother, with a smile, sorts out sheep wool, spins it, or knits socks and mittens. Her face shines with kindness. Also, she loves it when the house is clean, and she scrubs the floor, on her knees with a wet rag, and scrapes off the specks of dirt stuck to the bumpy floorboards with her fingernails. I sit cross-legged on the bench while she cleans. To avoid taking the garbage out of the house, she burns it in the woodstove.

More than anything, my grandma is afraid of the census. When it happens (in my lifetime, it was in 1970), she leaves the apartment and stays out.

Surprisingly, it was my grandmother with whom I made my most distant journeys; we traveled to Luhansk, Ukraine. I distinctly remember getting lost during one of these trips. There were three of us: my grandmother, Uncle Oleg (I call him Uncle Kaleka[5]), and myself. We were waiting for a train in the marble hall of Kazansky Station in Moscow. Grandma fell asleep, and I did not notice Uncle Oleg wandering off somewhere. I thought that he was nearby, and I followed a man who looked very much like him: he was of the same height and balding. I followed the man through endless underground

---

[5] *Kaleka* is translated from Russian as "physically disabled".

passages for a long time, believing, of course, that he was my uncle. Finally, the man approached a soda machine, dropped in a coin, and filled a glass with a fizzy drink. I came closer to him and asked for a drink. He turned around. When I saw his surprised and even somewhat distorted face, I immediately came to my senses (it remains possible that I was sleeping with my eyes open, and that I was sleepwalking). The man left, and I was alone in the middle of a hall. I started crying. It was either Yaroslavsky or Leningradsky Station. I was taken to the children's office of the railroad police. I said that I had come from Kazansky Station, and a woman in civilian clothes volunteered to take me back and asked the officers not to open a case on me.

When we returned to Kazansky Station, my grandmother had already woken up and was nervously circling the huge hall.

> *I saw your face in the silver oval*
> *of your smile and straight hair*
> *Again at the shimmering station*
> *in the midst of bustle and rebellious tears...*

Sometimes, impulsively, I wrap my arms around my grandmother's neck and kiss her wrinkled cheek. Grandpa jokes, coughing and smoking a hand-rolled cigarette near the half-open firebox: "Just like monkeys," and Dad quips, "Will you bring Grandma with you when you go to the Army?" Sometimes he makes fun of my grandmother's name, but I don't understand why.

It is getting dark outside, and dusk fills our room. Grandma Lina, our neighbor from the first floor, often drops in on us in the evenings. Today, she sits with us and drinks tea, telling spooky stories about some extraordinary animals. These bloodthirsty huge beasts look like diplodocus, and they are taller than our two-story building. I feel like they live somewhere nearby and can peek into our window at any moment. The residents of the surrounding streets (besides ours, there are also neighboring streets, named Krivaya Street and Belaya Street) love to make up all sorts of tales and pass them around. Movies are fuel for their myths; it is notable that *One Million B. C.* is currently shown in the theater on White Lake. I can't separate reality from legend and feel scared in the silence that follows.

Grandma makes crepes on Butter Week. I love crepes and my mom loves them, too. She often says the words "crap" and "badge".[6] I also say this, "Mom, I want a badge!" Our whole family is sitting at the table and eating crepes. Grandpa hiccups loudly. Remembering Pushkin, I exclaim, "Have you eaten too many crepes,[7] Grandpa?" I ask him why he is bald. Grandpa replies that Grandma made crepes on his head. I understand that this is a joke, but I still don't get an answer to my question. I wonder if it's possible to get an answer to any question?

I like different smells and tastes that others may not find appealing. What could be tastier than cod liver oil if Mom serves it in a tablespoon over a crust of lightly salted rye bread! Sometimes my grandmother cooks pies with onions and eggs or stewed guelder rose berries. Every summer my grandfather brings this berry from the forest. We sort it, and my grandmother fills a pot with guelder rose berries, sprinkles a little sugar on top, and puts it into the stove overnight. The berry gets stewed until morning, emitting a wonderful aroma. At some point, after my binky was thrown into the stove, I began to think that the sulfurous and acrid smell of burnt rubber was disgusting. Since then, I have not been able to drink milk from a clear glass. If it is really necessary, I will drink it from a mug in large sips, closing my eyes in disgust and dreaming about new archaeological excavations in the gully.

Everyone in our family has a pair of felt winter boots. In the winter, felt boots, called *pimy*, get worn out quickly, probably

---

[6] Pronunciation of Russian words meaning "badge" and "slut" has some similarity: *blyakha* and *blyad'*; this is similar to English when some people use shoot instead shit.

[7] Pronunciation of Russian words meaning "crepes" and "henbane" are pretty similar: *blini* and *beleni*.

because we wear them until summer and rarely use galoshes. I don't even remember seeing galoshes in our house. To sew felt boots, one needs shoe-thread. My grandfather makes the shoe-thread himself by unraveling an old retired fire hose. He pulls a durable thread from this hose several times through a lump of tar, which makes the thread waterproof. I observe his work closely. For repairs, he cuts a piece of felt from the top of an old felt boot in the shape of a heel or a toe. Then he puts the new part and the leaky part together and pokes holes in them with an awl and then stitches them to each other with the shoe-thread along the edge of the patch. Finally, he trims the patch to the size of the sole with a sharp knife.

My grandfather often sits by the stove and smokes tobacco. First, of course, he rolls up rectangular pieces of newspaper, fills them with shag tobacco from his oil-soaked tobacco pouch and glues them into tubes with saliva. Then he chain-smokes one hand rolled cigarette after another, blowing smoke into the door of the stove that's left ajar. A second-hand smoker, I am completely saturated with smoke, and when I visit my parents for the weekend in their home (it doesn't feel like my home, yet) in the new neighborhood, my clothes smell strongly of tobacco.

One day, my dad gave me a toy vehicle with a missile (perhaps a prototype of the future surface-to-air missile "BUK"). Compress the spring, and the missile would launch off the platform at a high speed. I began to look for a target, and Dad gave me one. When my grandfather once again sat down by the stove, I began to shoot at his hand that was holding the smoldering cigarette. Grandpa tolerated this for a time, and then pulled a leather belt from the belt loops on his pants and chased me around the table, spraying spit. I was scared and burst out crying.

When my grandfather is angry with someone, he grumbles with annoyance, "What a brat, eh!" or "Pipsqueak!" He only had a couple of years of schooling, and can read only haltingly.

At bedtime, I sometimes ask my grandfather to tell me a fairy tale, and he always tells his version of the same tale, a story about a crippled bear. He is missing one paw; in place of it, there is a wooden prosthesis, which the bear cut out from a linden tree for himself. Recently, I learned that this tale is called "Skeerly".

Before leaving on a hunt, my grandfather carefully presses primer into the cardboard ammo cartridges for his double-barreled shotgun and leaves the shot and gunpowder to add in later, once he arrives at his village of Milonovka. When it's just him and me at home, he plays like a child and shows me funny things. He closes up the hole for the primer with a soft bread crumb and inserts the sharp end of a knife into it. Holding the knife vertically by the handle with two fingers, Grandpa holds it at arm's length and lets go. The knife falls on a metal sheet nailed to the floor near the firebox of the woodstove. The primer explodes with a crack, spraying sparks. Grandpa runs around the room in excitement and eventually comes up with a new game. Instead of the knife, he takes a pointed sharp nail, attaches it to a large goose feather (Grandma uses it to spread butter on pies), carefully sticks the nail into the bread crumb in the primer and, standing in the doorway, throws this pro-jectile across the length of the room. The primer explodes be-tween the windowsill and the chest of drawers. He repeats the procedure. A humble student, I sit on the bench and watch this game with fascination.

My grandfather fought in the war, and it left him with two shrapnel scars: one is on his shoulder, and the other on his head. Due to congenital ptosis, his left eye is always slightly squinted. But he tells me that it is because he spent a lot of time looking through rifle sights. He never talks about the war, and only sighs heavily, "Oh, Grandson, Grandson..." But he never tells his story.

Striking a match, inhaling cigarette smoke into his lungs and releasing it into the open door of the stove, threading a coarse thread into the eye of the needle, inserting the primer into a cartridge, carrying buckets of water on the yoke up the snow-covered steps, reading haltingly, shaving with an open razor, and praying, my grandfather lives in his wisdom, still unfathomable for me, and all the while coughing and saying every now and then: "Oh, Grandson, Grandson." This wisdom, during the fighting at the frontlines, allowed him to go way beyond good and evil and to return.

Once, my grandfather recited a poem from memory:

> *"The smell of hay is on the field,*
> *and singing as they go*
> *the women toss the heavy yield*
> *and spread it row by row.*
> *And yonder where the hay is dry*
> *each man his forkful throws,*
> *until the wagon loaded high*
> *is like a house that grows..."[8]*

The scenery described by the Russian poet Apollon Maykov is apparently very close to my grandfather.

Grandpa keeps his medals in a red box. I like to peruse them. There are all kinds of medals, but there is none "For the Capture of Berlin". Recently, I asked after these medals, and one of the adults replied, "Well, you played with them and probably lost them." This was a shock to me. I never ask again, and only many years later I will come across them and realize with relief that they have never really been lost.

A day calendar hangs on the wall. There, several days of the year are marked in red, and the rest are black. Usually, my grandfather tears off the page of yet another day past from the calendar and thoroughly reads, coughing, "Sunrise is at ..., sunset is at ... The length of the daylight is ... " Occasionally, he tears off several pages at once or forgets to do so for several days. Or maybe he just leaves for the village, or goes hunting... So there is no proper succession of days in our house, and sometimes the next day does not come for a long time, so I live

---

[8] Translated by Frances Cornford, an English poet, and Esther Polianowsky Salaman, a Russian-born Jewish writer and physicist.

as if suffering from a disease in a void.

So, I am holding a thermometer in my armpit. The mercury jumps to the highest mark. Dad says that if medicine didn't exist, I would not have survived the pressure of natural selection. As soon as I get sick, the children's doctor Galina Kurkina drops by, and my treatment begins. She is a renowned doctor, and once we were even filmed together for a news program.

I'm on bed rest. Fairytale Russia spreads on a tapestry before my eyes. I lie in bed facing the wall and follow the lines of Three Bogatyrs' horses with my finger. Alyosha Popovich has a mysterious horse. The Bogatyrs can do everything, and I beg them to give me strength, pulling out a few threads from the tapestry. In the evenings, fragments of fairy tales reach me through the veil of consciousness from the mouth of my mother. I like the tale about Ivan Tsarevich[9] and the Gray Wolf most of all. As soon as I feel my strength returning, I start building with toy blocks. I even have a topographic tower of about three feet in height (or length, it depends on the way I play). There is a ladder on the tower, which I climb with two fingers acting as legs. This tower was given to me by auntie Sveta Vyugova. She lives just below us and works at the Topographic College on

---

[9] *Tsarevich* is translated as "prince" in Russian; namely, tsarevich is a son of a *tsar*.

"Rozochka" (that's what we call the Roza Luxemburg Street). When my father crosses the Lethe River, his friends will give me the new address of Svetlana Arkadyevna and ask me to inform her about his departure personally. I will go and bring her this tragic news. Svetlana Arkadyevna will start crying, "She nagged him to death... tortured him..."

There is a small hill nearby. This is where I first learned to ski. I had wooden skis with leather binding that fitted to my felt boots. First my grandfather, and then my dad taught me to go down this hill. But it's more fun to go sledding down another, even steeper one, on the nearby Lermontov Street, right behind the Berezina bath-house.

I once went there to sled (naturally, the strap of my sled was made of kerosene wick) and ran into Tanya Okamova, with whom I would often play in our yard. She is beautiful, like all girls, but I don't need anyone else, just her. How huge was my disappointment when I saw that Tanya was sledding with an-

other boy, a boy older than me! I felt so miserable... This episode coincided with the fact that Tanya began to spend less and less time with me after school. Eventually, she completely forgot about me. I felt out of sorts, and life did not appeal to me. I withdrew into my shell more and more, daydreaming about permafrost and mountain peaks and losing touch with reality.

Years will pass. Getting ready to go on a taiga expedition and having already packed some supplies, I'll walk into the shoe store at the intersection of Academic Street and John Lennon Avenue. Tanya Okamova (or maybe she has a different surname already) works there as a sales associate. I will choose a pair of high-top sneakers, and Tanya will tell me, "You will feel every pebble through such a thin sole." These words will be the last that I will ever hear from her, and I will read the *word "shoes" on the store name as "love"*.[10] She did not know that, where I would be going, there were no pebbles, only swamp. I wanted to explain it to her, but it was no longer im-

---

[10] A quote from the novel *A School for Fools* by Sasha Sokolov. Pronunciation of Russian words meaning "shoes" and "love" has some resemblance: *obuv'* and *lubov'*. Translator Alexander Boguslawski used "gloves" instead of "shoes" to show this similarity in his English translation of the novel.

portant. Over the following years, the formidable gully in our yard will have turned into a canyon on the other side of the Earth, and I, like Benjamin Button, will have inevitably approached my childhood.

> Good night again I wish to you.
> We have an eternity left to live
> maybe even two eternities.
> Morning flies into infinity when
> you open wide the window to the sky,
> and with a slight body movement,
> you collect a hand-fan of hair.
> Of acacia and aniline color
> the dawn is already burning in the distance,
> and somewhere in the nearest canyon
> time floats on the river.

Like Leonardo five hundred years ago, I did not notice the night pass. The stars winked out, and a pink glow lighted the tiled ledges of the roof of your house. Sasha Sokolov will say, "*Folks, love day more than night!*" There is something positive in this appeal, and perhaps even a desperate awakening to eternal values. Still, I like a moonlit night (but maybe only on this night).

After re-reading the last part of my poem, I burn it and scatter the ashes in the canyon, where the restless sound of the river is heard. Then, remembering the advice of Dr. Kurkina, I restore the text, reconnecting with myself for a short time. This time does not belong to me, it flows and floats away into eternity.

Soon I will go to school where I will learn discipline and maybe even run cross-country races that will build up my health. Mom is already sewing a bag for the change of shoes, and I dream of a bicycle with a bell, of working for the benefit of mankind, and putting a weathervane on the balcony of the third floor. My mother bought me colored (that is, magical) blocks with letters and pictures on them. Vowels and consonants. I'm trying to put these blocks together, like a mosaic, and form words and even sentences:

Az. *Thin curves of water avens:*
spring and autumn in a sweaty fist.
Buki. *The Little Prince, wizard of the fields,*
is sad without people in the fog of lightning.
He breaks off the thorns with his thin hand;
He is the Executor of the dream for earthly life.
Vede. *Waiting for my ascent into the cold of the*
distant and beautiful glaciers with or without a cross.
(Does it matter?) You will call me to this path with a smile,
and my heart will clench from the lack of oxygen
on the white peak.
Glagol.
Dobro.
Yeste.
Zhivite.
Zemlya...

And so it goes.

Along the Northern Branch

The train is coming... The northern branch,
A branch of acacia or, perhaps, lilac...

Sasha Sokolov

Sometimes you may hear in a conversation that a train travels on a loop: for example, when you need to interpret something important in a different way or when talking about the Moscow Subway, or during children's play, when a toy train with small cars circles on its track.

When I was young, the train headed north and came back. But the people who returned, arrived changed.

In late August, my dad and I were going berry picking. I was 15 years old, and Dad decided I was old enough to come along... And I was going into the Siberian taiga for the first time. The nearest settlement was at least twenty-five miles away. Our journey here seemed long to me.

We traveled by train along the Northern branch during the early evening and all night. The train car was packed with berry-pickers and their huge boxes, called *gorboviks*.

In the overcrowded train car, my dad helped me squeeze onto an upper berth. I covered my face with a windbreaker and, pulling my knees up to my chin, soon fell asleep.

At five in the morning, my dad shook me awake and said into my ear, "Get ready quickly! We're getting close!" I wiped my glasses, climbed down from the berth and, half-awake, located my boots. It was still dark outside.

The wheels were making the familiar "clickety-clack" noise on the tracks, when someone pulled the emergency brake, and

the train stopped abruptly. The berry-pickers had been standing by and rushed to the exit. They let go of the handrails and
jumped from the train steps like parachutists into the darkness of the taiga morning. Within minutes, they all tumbled
out into the vast expanse. Most of them went along the railway
embankment to the signal lights at the crossing gate; apparently, that was the main road to the logging site.

"We have our own spot," said my dad and waved his hand
over his left shoulder.

We crossed the tracks and plunged deep into the forest
along a trail which was barely visible in the morning twilight.
I plodded behind, now and then bumping into my dad's aluminum box.

With the first light, the trail turned down into a lowland.

At the turn, my dad stopped, walked up to a lonely pine tree, and began to count his steps.

"It should be here!" he shouted.

We threw some branches to the side and pulled two light barbells out of the grass. There were two pairs of small aluminum wheels with a flange. They rotated freely on well-oiled bearings mounted on long metal rods.

A quarter of an hour later we came to a narrow-gauge railway track, which was used for transportation of felled timber. We found some wood planks in a pile of garbage near the railroad. We put together a platform and nailed the rods to it to make the chassis. We put this mini-cart on the rails and climbed onto it with our stuff. To avoid injuring our hands, we put on canvas mittens (*verkhonki*) and began to push with poles off the rail embankment and ties. Slowly, we gained speed. The sound of wheels became more frequent: "clickety-clack, clickety-clack... click-clack, click-clack... click-clack, click-clack, click-clack..." Our rail cart swayed slightly because of the rough tracks. It felt like we were on a raft with our poles tilted forward.

"Vissarionov Bor[11]!" Dad declared. His gray hair, peeking from under a funny beanie hat, fluttered in the wind.

I was gazing around. Dense mast-height forest alternated with clear-cut patches. Rail tracks often lost their continuity, as if in perfect harmony with the landscape. Sometimes the joints were close to the wheels' diameter, and sometimes we inevitably crashed. Fortunately, we never got injured. Sometimes we had to carry the cart because in some places rails were missing entirely.

We traveled along the narrow-gauge railway for more than twenty miles until there were no more tracks. Saplings fought their way through the remains of the embankment. We carried the cart to the side and covered it with moss.

We started walking along the swamp, following the compass to the northeast.

An hour later, lingonberry bushes began to appear on pillows of moss. I bent down to have a good look at the leaf pattern of this amazing berry. The top of the leaves was glossy and with black spots on the underside.

Dad wiped sweat off his face with a sleeve of his windbreaker and ordered:

"A breather!"

We sat down on a fallen tree trunk. We fished out cucumbers, hard-boiled eggs, bread, and water from our boxes and had a quick meal.

---

[11] *Bor* means a coniferous forest. Vissarionov Bor is a forest near Bely Yar, a settlement in the Verkhneketsky District of Tomsk Region, Russia.

"Alright, that's enough being lazy. Time to get to work!" Dad commanded.

He showed me how to use the scoop. Then he adjusted his shoulder strap and moved toward the pine brushwood.

Closer to noon, I came across a narrow forest glade with lingonberry shrubs all over. I dropped the box from my shoulders and, now unburdened, got absorbed in the berry picking: I was really diligent and kept my eyes on the berries. I noted one berry shrub as I harvested another, repeating the same movement with the scoop.

After a couple of hours, I came to the edge of the glade, where I found a large coil of rusted barbed wire next to an old uprooted tree. A huge pine tree grew three yards away. It had an old notch, some carved digits, and letters that spelled "TAL".[12]

"Why is this here?" I wondered aloud, pointing at the coils of wire.

---

[12] The abbreviation for Tomsk-AsinLag, a part of GULAG, a system of Soviet labor camps and prisons that from 1920s to mid-1950s housed millions of political prisoners and criminals.

"It looks like they wanted to build a camp."

"What kind of camp?"

"A prison camp," Dad muttered.

Gazing gloomily into the distance, he said:

"Someone happened to be here, at the logging site. The felled timber was taken out on a horse-drawn narrow-gauge railway... In the 1930s, they arrested anyone and everyone..."

"But why?"

Dad did not answer; he had already turned away and gone to the nearest spruce grove, and the brushwood snapped under his feet.

I carefully looked around. There were only moss-covered hummocks. I kicked one, then another... The toe of my boot sank into rotten stumps. Ants swarmed in the exposed dust...

By evening it began to drizzle. We came up to a creek; a small hillock rose behind it — this was an excellent place for an overnight stay. We built a shelter under a sprawling spruce and spread fir branches on the ground for a floor. We opened a couple of cans of fish. Dad pulled out a flask of alcohol, measured several caps into his glass, and, without diluting with water, drank it in one gulp. A minute later, he cheered up and began to tell a story about his time working as a movie projector operator in his youth and driving a horse-drawn movie theater from village to village. One day, the film with one of Stalin's speeches got ripped.

"I nearly crapped my pants while I was fixing this film," Dad said through laughter.

Then he recalled last summer in the taiga with his brother. They picked berries near the Bear Cape and got lost on their way back to their motorboat. They wandered around the taiga for three days. They ate only berries until they finally found the river. I didn't hear him tell how they had figured out whether to search for their boat upstream or downstream. I'd already fallen asleep to the sound of drizzling rain.

In the morning, I woke up to the courtship call of a wood grouse. I scrambled out of the shelter and pulled on my boots. My dad was not at the campsite. His crouched figure could be seen on the other side of the swampy hollow. He was picking berries. So I ran to the swamp to find the place where I heard the courtship call. I wiped my fogged-up glasses and saw a large bird in the middle of a swamp on a lone dry tree. It was the wood grouse.

By lunchtime, I picked enough berries to fill half of the box. Dad's box was almost full. We had to go back, to be in time for the train departure, and the way to the railway station was long!

On the way back, we rode a few miles longer upon a narrow-gauge railway that was closer to the station. We dismantled the rail cart, threw the wheels under a snag and covered them with bark; they would be useful when we would come back cranberry picking in September.

I wanted to return to the taiga again; to walk through the quaking bog and unroll my wading boots and fall onto my knees into the soft sphagnum mat...

By the time the train arrived, it was already dark. The train brakes clunked. Shoving one another aside, people with heavy boxes rushed to the train cars. Dad pushed me to the nearest door. I grabbed the handrails and jumped onto the step first; my dad fought his way up behind me.

Minutes later, the train car was packed full and buzzing with male voices. Some people remained standing in the vestibule. I sat down on the edge of a lower berth, crossed my forearms on the lid of the *gorbovik*, rested my head on them, and fell asleep.

In the morning, the streets of our town were flashing past outside the window. The train stopped. We got off onto the railway platform.

It was not far from the railway station to home. First, we passed through the railway station neighborhood for about half a mile; next, we walked along the railway tracks for approximately ten minutes.

We made our way past the prefabricated five-story apartment buildings. Two drunken young men were having a noisy conversation at one of the entrances; they were slapping each other on the shoulders. Dad shot some innocent joke at them.

They didn't like it, so one of them ran up to us and hit me in the chest. I lost my balance and fell. I could not get up. The other man was standing in a puddle of beer and waving his arms, keeping my dad from coming to my aid. The first man continued to kick me, aiming for my head. I covered my face and glasses with my hands and curled up. Almost all of his hits landed on my forearms.

"What did the kid do to you?" yelled my dad in a strange hoarse voice.

Fear pulled me down like a whirlpool. The box with berries was still on my shoulders.

Finally, the men left. Dad helped me up, and I saw the light. We continued walking on the creosote-soaked ties along the railroad tracks. I trudged in silence, snuffling quietly and unable to feel any pain in my numb limbs; that came later. I held my glasses with my trembling hands: the temples were bent.

Soon we reached our neighborhood, called Experimental Field. The sign on the outermost five-story apartment building announced, not without irony: "Building #1, Berry Street". The cold wind squalled and plucked the first shriveled leaves off the poplars. I was astonished: they were green when we left for the taiga.

I followed my dad down the street. He asked me not to tell my mother about the incident. I said nothing. I was remembering how we walked through the ginger peat bogs and shrub forest and picked berries. The berries relocated from the taiga to our boxes. The berries were red and already releasing their juices.

The next morning, I woke up from a deep sleep.

Mom suggested that I deliver a jar of lingonberries to Ilya, my friend and next-door neighbor. Ilya and I played chess together on rare occasions.

I went down one floor to Ilya's and, over a cup of tea, I told him about my discovery of barbed wire in the taiga. He thought about it and then promised to take me to the greenhouse where meetings of the Cultural Club were held from time to time.

"At a greenhouse?" I was surprised. "That's unusual!"

"Bogdan works there as a watchman. Actually, he is a sociologist at the university."

At the appointed time, we hurried to the greenhouse. Of course we did! The greenhouse reminded us of our childhood and my first visit to the botanical gardens. There was even a photo from that trip in my family album: roots of tropical trees crawling towards each other, vines wrapping around the trunks, and a toddler underneath a palm tree: me.

I went, impatient and excited. I believed that this visit would bring me an understanding of something important: it was as if I, not Vera Pavlovna, had the dream[13] that apparently only in a greenhouse can you grow such *ears*.

Flowers were grown in the greenhouse. In anticipation of the discussion, two young people walked along the garden beds: asters grew in the left row, lilies in the right.

"The leaf is good, and the flower is good. Women will be happy. Everything will be fine," Vassily said.

---

[13] The 4th Dream of Vera Pavlovna in the novel *What Is to Be Done?* by Nikolay Chernyshevsky, a Russian literary and social critic, journalist, novelist, democrat, and socialist philosopher.

I couldn't tell if he was serious.

Bogdan stood next to the empty seedling pots. He held a notebook with lecture notes and was preparing for his speech. Six more people showed up.

I do not remember at all what was discussed at that meeting. It was hot and unbearably stuffy, and I wanted to leave as soon as possible because of that.

That winter I visited the Club's discussions a couple more times. That's where I first learned about Aleksandr Solzhenitsyn and Varlam Shalamov, but I wasn't allowed to borrow any books: they had yet to make sure that I could be trusted. No one really knew the history of the construction of the Northern rail branch and the prison camp; instead, they spoke about loftier matters most of the time.

The spring of the leap year of 1980 came. In March, Vassily was reported to the authorities by his ex-wife. She uncovered and reported his network of acquaintants and the list of foreign and dissident print-outs (*samizdat*). The greenhouse was searched, and books and photocopies were confiscated. Searches were also made at people's homes. The local KGB[14] initiated the *"greenhouse case"*. Bogdan and Vassily were dismissed from their jobs. Ilya advised me to leave town for a while.

I had not visited my grandfather in his village for a long time. The village sat at that same Northern rail branch.

I got off the train at the familiar railway stop: there was a wooden platform and a ticket booth. The lone railway pointsman in a bright vest walked along the railway track, waving a flag. After passing the treeless buffer zone, I turned onto a country road.

Spring arrived early that year. Snow had melted in the open places; dirty snow piles covered with needles and rotten leaves could be seen in the hollows and in the shade of trees. The ruts on the road were full of snowmelt. There was nobody to give me a ride, but that was fine. I walked slowly, remembering

---

[14] KGB means Committee for State Security in the USSR.

these places of my childhood. At this very turn, my grandfather broke a stem off a cow parsnip, peeled it and gave me a bit to taste; after that he said, half-seriously, "As long as there is cow parsnip and goutweed, we won't starve." Behind this hillock, we walked along the roadside, and sometimes we would wander into the forest, hunting for mushrooms. Here was a turn to Malinovka, a neighboring village. Further on, a ramshackle bridge. The right bank of the river was densely overgrown with willow shrubs. Local boys fished for graylings.

Last time I was here, my grandfather coughed lightly but persistently, saying over and over for no apparent reason, "Oh, Grandson, Grandson..."

I hadn't seen my grandpa for two years. What was he like now?

The road, full of potholes and bumps, approached the outskirts. Soon a pond appeared. An old silo rose behind the pond. Its black silhouette was reflected in the cold water. I went fishing here for the first time. Grandpa made rods out of willow twigs, and we went fishing on a small cape overgrown with reeds. I watched the cork float for a long time; it was getting blown away by the wind to the bushes over and over again. Suddenly, the float disappeared under water, and the fishing line pulled taut. I pulled on the fishing rod and dragged a crucian carp ashore. Grandpa saw my catch, came up and grunted that it was time to go back home. All the way back, he was begging me to tell grandma Zhenya that it was him, and not me, who had caught the fish.

As a child, I learned my grandfather's story. During WWII, he returned home emaciated. People who lived in town were also starving, so he went to the village in the north to gain some weight. He lived with the family of Zhenya, a first cousin of his wife. Zhenya's husband was killed during the Winter War. My grandfather began to divide his time between the two homes, and after my grandmother passed away, he permanently moved to the village.

And this next hillock was very familiar; here was the log cabin with sagging window shutters. Turning onto a barely noticeable trail, I went up to the outbuildings. A goose hissed to warn me, and then a dog barked... The wet soil near the barn was dotted with bird droppings. There was a bloodstained ax on the porch. Pushing the door hard with my shoulder, I stumbled into the warm cabin.

My grandpa was sitting by the window, gazing in delight at the bouquet of blooming pussy willow branches. Once he saw me, he raised his eyebrows in surprise, jumped up and shouted around the woodstove, "Zhenya, put the *samovar*[15] on! Grandson is here!"

I walked forward and saw grandma Zhenya on a small bench in the corner of the hut. She was plucking a chicken.

"My Lord! Yegor!" grandma Zhenya gasped in surprise.

Clasping her hands, she bustled around the house. Sounds came randomly from her toothless mouth. "You're all grown!" Her speech was mushy, and I could barely make out the words.

I smiled and took a jar of lingonberries out of my backpack: it was the last batch from previous year's picking.

After a late dinner, they prepared a daybed for me, and I sank into a feather comforter. Above the bed there was a tapestry depicting spotted deer near a lake. A wood grouse's tail hung like a fan on the opposite wall. I looked at this hunting trophy of my grandfather for a long time and thought about the events of the past year before falling asleep.

I lived in this nearly desolate village for a week. There was a score of houses, and half of them were empty. The only street was quiet and sleepy. Only once did I see an old man with a walking stick; people said that he had injured his leg at a logging site when he was young.

In the mornings, I lay for a long time on the daybed and daydreamed, like Oblomov.[16] There was nothing to read in the house, except for a day calendar. I was bored and, on the sev-

---

[15] *Samovar* is a metal container traditionally used to heat and boil water in Russia.

[16] Oblomov is the protagonist of a novel of the same name (1859) by Ivan A. Goncharov, a Russian novelist.

enth evening, declared that the next day I would go back to town.

My grandfather was sad. Then he asked for my help in making butter, and, wiping his bald head with a handkerchief, said slowly in a low voice:

"You'll bring a gift of butter to your mother... She's completely forgotten me... I was waiting for her to visit on Easter..."

Grandma Zhenya got some cream from the cellar. I began to beat it in a wooden churn, a narrow tub held together by two steel hoops. Sitting on a low stool, I repeated the same movement monotonously. Countless times, I lifted the chiseled handle and quickly dipped it into the springy cream. I was exhausted by the time I felt the handle of the churn push against something solid. Opening the lid, I saw a shapeless lump of sun-colored butter.

Grandma Zhenya walked over to me. I heard her gasping and making sounds of approval. I was so excited!

The next morning, Grandpa saw me off on the village outskirts. He was coughing heavily. Tears flowed from his inflamed eyes and down his stubble-covered cheeks.

All the way to the country road, I often turned back and waved to Grandpa, for as long as I could see his lonely figure.

The train arrived into town late in the evening. After stepping out on the railway platform, I crossed the square and fearlessly strode through the deserted railway station neighborhood.

Two young men stood under the canopy of one of the

building entrances. I nodded to them. I passed through the yard, turned toward the railroad tracks and then proceeded walking on the ties. I proudly carried a willow branch in my backpack.

Red semaphore lights flickered in the distance. A rusty train car stood still at a dead end. A locomotive whistle sounded. The railroad tracks squealed at a curve. They had been hardened in the foundries of a bygone era.

Under the Riemann's Dome

Tonight, heavy rain cleared the ash from the air. The small team of bio-volcanologists was finally headed to the volcano. There were three of us: Vianor, Elektra, and I. We walked along the edge of a forest that had perished in the pyroclastic flow. Charred and skinned tree trunks still smoldered in the valley. The previously spectacular landscape had turned into a rocky desert. *Yes, life is destroyed, but somewhere under our feet, it is being born again now*, I thought.

Three hours later, we reached the base of a new volcano: a subordinate one and so far unnamed. The volcano roared continuously. Lava, flying out of its crater, broke into fragments in the air, which were falling like little bombs, or clots of the earth's blood. The orange orb of the sun hovered like a mirage to the right of the volcano. Our shadows, disproportionately long and with strange humps, were cast along the slope.

We pulled tools from our backpacks and took samples of the still hot rock fragments. Vianor observed the air for safety reasons while I knocked off pieces of the scorching lava that we found in the funnels and placed them into sterile capsules.

Soon the eruption intensified, and we headed back towards the camp. We walked through a valley dotted with steam vents, which spewed sour sulfur dioxide gas. To the northwest, the snow-white dome of the main volcano was visible in the haze. My companions hastily put on masks, but I lingered and breathed in quite a bit of gas, and felt unwell. I felt a little dizzy, and reminiscences of my youth arose in my memory: the common yard, my old friends, the teachers...

During my years of undergraduate studies and postgraduate work assignment, I happened to live in a new district, built in the suburbs next to a vegetable warehouse. My one-bedroom apartment was on the third floor of a panel building that almost touched the corner of the neighboring five-story apartment building. Back in the day, these tall buildings with flat roofs were erected all over the country.

One September evening, I was at home, pondering over a notebook, and planning my academic paper. The sunset shone brightly outside the window. I went out onto the balcony to get some fresh air and looked down.

Yelagin appeared from the narrow passage between the buildings and headed for his entrance. He carried a leather briefcase that almost touched the ground. Yelagin was a "little person", or, simply, a dwarf. Other kids never laughed at him, only watched him solemnly as he walked by. I often dropped by the second-hand bookstore where he worked. Yelagin usually sat at the back of the store, surrounded by massive stacks of books. High, stucco-molding arcs kept shelves in alignment; books stood there in close ranks. In this interior, he looked like a gnome from a fairytale. One day, when I was a teenager, I went to his house and was astonished to spot a human skull on the small table in the hallway. I was in a daze. I swallowed hard and left quickly. I still don't understand why this scared me so much. Five years later, while studying anatomy in my first year of Medical University, I could easily hold an anatomical specimen of a skull in my hands.

I told about these events to my friend Ilya, my next-door neighbor, when one quiet evening we were reminiscing about the good old days at a couple of games of chess. By then, our favorite place, a wooden table in the yard next to a sprawling willow-tree, no longer existed, and we sat on a bench under the concrete canopy of the entryway.

Ilya listened to me attentively and then, making a strong emphasis on "m", he said, "M-maybe this skull is a reminder of the inevitability of death, *memento mori*?"

"For every guest? I can only imagine..."

"And he works with old books, where the passions of the ancestors are digitized," Ilya continued.

As a child, he stuttered more and was ashamed of his speech impediment. Years passed, and Ilya became quite a mature young man. The dimples in his once plump cheeks disappeared. He had already graduated from a Technical College and had a job: he waited for visitors at the counter of his booth.

After the chess games, we shook hands, and Ilya disappeared into the dark doorway of the entrance. That was our last meeting.

In the 1990s, a market appeared where the vegetable warehouse used to be, right behind my apartment building. Ilya's mother set up a vending booth there. Previously, she had worked at the warehouse and thus was able to privatize a small area of the marketplace. But some people were jealous of her spot and her success.

Ilya helped his mother with sales. When there were no buyers, he took advantage of his free time and played chess, coming up with new combinations.

One fateful morning, he stood in for his mother, but forgot his chess set and decided to run back home for it. Ilya went up to his apartment on the second floor. Suddenly, the doorbell rang. His mother hurried to the door and cracked it open, and at that moment an ax broke through the security chain. Ilya stepped in front of his mother to shield her, but this did not save either of them — in a moment it was all over. Gasoline splashed out of a plastic bottle, a burning match was flicked into the room, and the metal door was shut.

When I heard about the tragedy from neighbors, I walked out of the house and got on a trolleybus. Standing by the window on the back deck, I watched people disappear in the distance. A young man in a greasy shirt crouched next to me. He held a plastic bag filled with gasoline and from time to time opened it and greedily sucked in the fumes. The guy's stare was vacant. None of the passengers paid him any mind.

I got off at the terminus, the Le Corbusier quarter, and became a pedestrian.

It was May. Leaves had already appeared on the trees. The scent of chokecherry blossoms filled the air. People were delighted with the awakening of life. Children played joyfully.

Ahead of me, a young couple was walking down the alley, and as they passed a lonely tree with stubby bare branches, I overheard a bit of their conversation.

"The tree is dead," the man stated the obvious.

"Perhaps it may yet come back to life," the woman said.

"According to you, everything may come back to life," he muttered.

"And you rush to bury everything," she said, taking his hand.

I stopped, thoughtfully watching them walk away: she was dressed in light clothes, and he was in dark.

That year I decided to become a medical biologist and study growth-promoting substances. I wanted to understand why organisms grow, and how to use scientific knowledge to help patients restore health. It is possible that my acquaintance with Yelagin and Ilya subconsciously influenced my choice.

I was lucky with my mentors. Many of them were great teachers. I learned from one famous academician that during WWII, a professor invented a recipe for a healing ointment to treat the wounded. The ointment was made at a meat-packing plant using cattle embryos. A huge homogenizer stirred the embryos, turning them into a clay-like paste with a strong morphogenetic field. In evacuation hospitals in Siberia, this substance was applied to mangled bodies, and the germplasm grew into the tissues, causing rapid regeneration. I was so impressed when I heard this that one day I had a dream, where this plasma filled the burning trenches, and activated the surviving genes. Skeletons grew muscles and

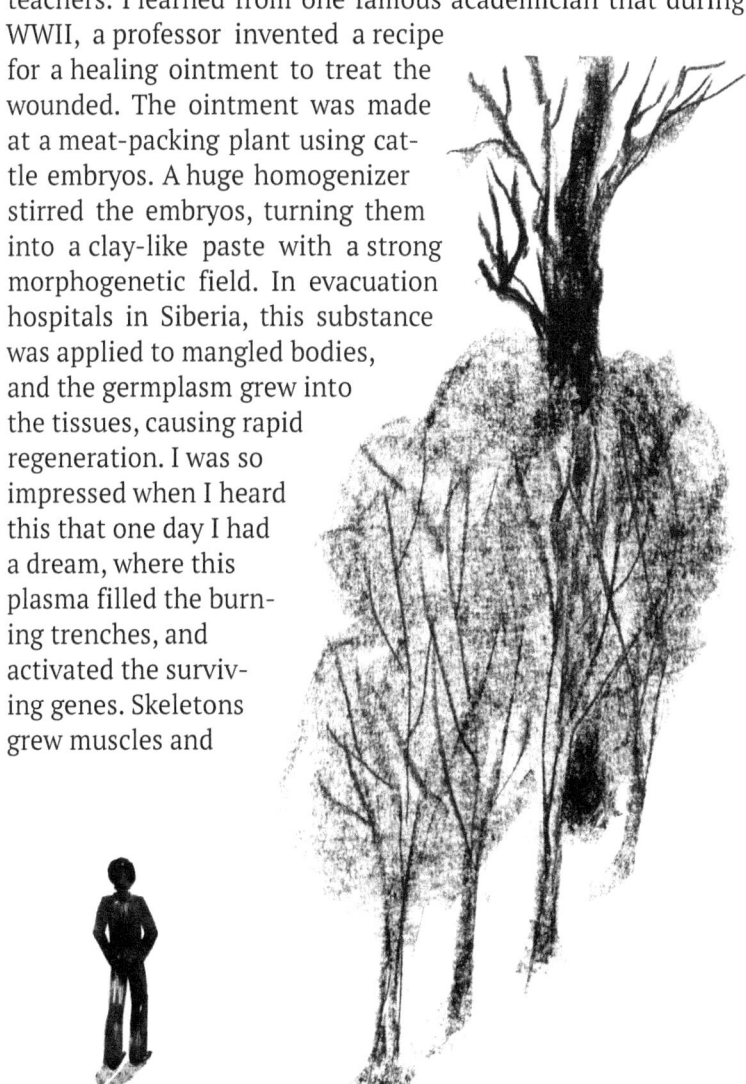

veins, and waves of convulsions ran through the bodies of the soldiers, reviving and resurrecting their bodies.

After classes, I used to go to the library and read books by Metchnikoff and Oparin and study works by Ilya Prigogine in synergetics. Then I would stay late into the night at the University, where my mentor, Professor Bogdanov, was working on the cultivation of human stem cells. But the cells did not develop without growth promoting substances, which are abundant in the tissues of embryos and their blood. Therefore, the Professor suggested that the students should go collect blood from the umbilical cords of newborns. My classmate Elektra and I volunteered for the next night shift.

Late that night, we put on medical gowns and were directed to one of the delivery rooms of the maternity hospital. While waiting for a woman in the last stage of labor, we sat down on a vacant hospital bench and looked around. Opposite us was the birthing bed. The cold light of fluorescent lamps gleamed on the blue wall tiles. Time went by. I held a rack with empty test tubes on my lap. To entertain Elektra, I told her a parable about an old digger who went underground to look for crystal nodules of young sprouts of embryonic life. The fractal nodules contained growth promoting substances, so they had a significant biotic potential, comparable only to the effects of the Water of Life.

After midnight, a woman in labor was brought to the ward. Her water had broken, and she cried out with every contraction. Then I heard the cry of the newly born baby. It was a pure revelation for me: *In the blink of an eye, a new human being appeared*! I stepped towards the mother, but the obstetrics nurse stopped me with a motion of his hand, grabbed my test tubes and began to fill them with blood from the cut umbilical cord. I stood, swaying, sweat on my forehead. I turned to look at Elektra for a second. She sat still on the cot, her profile as pale as that of a Greek statue.

Dawn was approaching when we left the hospital. To obtain serum, we had to sediment the blood clots via centrifugation, so we took a shortcut to the lab through a deserted city park.

The soft glow of the full moon illuminated the path and the young leaves of the trees. The branches cast bizarre delicate shadows. In the distance, a Devil's wheel[17] was silhouetted above the treetops of poplars. I was bewildered. Which of the two worlds was real? Was it there, at the hospital, where we had just witnessed the birth of a new human being, or here, in the park?

Suddenly Elektra asked: "Have you read *Moonlight* by Guy de Maupassant?"

"No, I haven't," I muttered, ashamed. "Why?"

"No reason," Elektra chuckled.

We crossed the park and reached a street. Gloomy houses with dark windows brooded over us. We walked in silence through this huge corridor. Gradually, the sky began to glow silver above our heads.

Soon, the vapors from the ammonia fumaroles brought me back to reality. We approached a stream of lava, and in some places a bright red glow could be seen through the cracks. A flock of birds warmed themselves near a stream. A few yards away, dusky-blue clay gurgled in small hollows.

Twilight came and we finally got to our tent, tired. We lit a fire. Vianor threw a lilac-colored wrap over Elektra's shoulders. They sat down by the fire and stared at it. I settled myself at some distance and, yet again, memories rushed in.

After graduating, I got a job at the Institute of Morphogenesis. One day, colleagues from a nearby city decided to test the anti-tumor properties of embryonic tissue and invited me to collaborate. We started with chicken embryos. I went to a poultry farm, bought a hundred fertilized eggs from the incubator and brought them to the lab. Elektra quickly cracked the eggshells and deftly removed the embryos using tweezers. I did this work slowly, wondering why an egg yields a bird which lays eggs again.

---

[17] In Russian, Devil's wheel is a kind of Ferris wheel.

We were well paid for the embryo extract that we had produced.

Later, I accidentally found out that my colleagues from that city were selling it to cancer patients. We were angry and decided to stay out of such temptations from then on. Elektra transferred to the Department of Chemistry. I felt down and got drunk. Vianor from an adjacent laboratory supported me when I almost completely stopped doing my research.

Vianor was developing energy cones. He created them from various materials containing, among other things, volcanic pumice stone.

"Life once originated in volcanoes," Vianor explained.

"You're too much of a dreamer!" I commented briefly, though I had already mentally built a logical chain: *dreamer—story—fiction—pseudoscience...* But I did not dare to pronounce the last word: I was afraid to offend him or to be wrong.

Vianor smiled and said with conviction, "I am sure that life begins with an irrational space," and after a pause he added, "Anyway, my cones improve metabolism."

Then he scratched the back of his head and launched into a detailed story about the German scientist Riemann, who lived in the 19th century. It turned out that this mathematician suggested that the geometry in the microcosm differed from the three-dimensional Euclidean geometry. At the end of his monologue, Vianor shared his innermost ideas:

"So, I think that the geometry in a living organism is also non-Euclidean! And my cones are effective because an elliptical Riemannian space is formed under them!"

A huge cone hung over Vianor's bed. "If ifs and buts were these cones, they would have a great harvest on the collective farms," his colleagues joked.

We started working together, and one day we placed stem cells with embryonic extract under one of the cones. In the experiment, we discovered that the new embryos started in the Petri dish, but their growth stopped after the first few cell divisions.

Vianor decided to go to a volcano and search for natural materials for improving his cones.

I thought, *Why does an organism need to take growth promoting substances from others each time they want to continue life? Isn't there any other way?*

While reading scientific works, I learned that fullerene carbon nanotubes could be the cradle of life on Earth, and I begged Vianor to take me on an expedition. Elektra joined us. That's how we all came to be here together.

The next day, the volcano fell still, and we climbed up to the crater. A strong wind was blowing at the top. I cautiously approached the edge and looked down. My head was spinning a little, as I had been afraid of heights since I was a child. The bottom was covered with slabs of solidified lava, and tendrils of yellowish gas rose from the walls of the crater. The distance from the edge to the bottom was like that from the balcony of a third floor to the ground. I remembered how, in the building across from mine, parents grounded their misbehaving daughter, locked her in the apartment, and went to work. The girl was my peer in eighth grade. Clinging to the railings of the balconies, she fearlessly descended from floor to floor...

I put on a mask and thermal protective overalls. I attached a safety rope. Then I began to slowly climb down into the dark inferno. Instinctively, I looked up and saw a large bird circling above the crater. The sun was dazzling at its zenith. It was hot, but the heat was not coming from the sun. It came from the depths of the Earth, from its womb.

I kept going down. Finally, I was close to the bottom, where lava was still bubbling in the cracks, and, with some difficulty, I took several samples.

That night, we gathered again at the camp by the fire.

After dinner, Vianor and Elektra disappeared into the tent. I kept looking in the direction of the new volcano and wondering whether someone should remain awake and stand watch, in case it woke up again.

The moon rose. The snow-covered dome of the progenitor volcano sparkled with turquoise. A long cloud of volcanic vapor shimmered in the valley. I was excited and stunned by what I saw. Then I smiled at my simple thought that, while searching for a scientific truth of the origin of life, I became like that abbot from Maupassant's short novel. I did read the story and knew what Elektra was referring to.

I opened a notebook and made notes on my observations. At the end, I added, "I want to name the new crater after Riemann."

Dark Room, Ginger Suitcase

I t was an early morning in July. Twilight still reigned over the third floor of a five-story apartment building. In the far corner of the room, under a thin sheet, slept a middle-aged man named Gleb. Now, he opened his eyes, stretched, and scratched a heel on the arm of the sofa. His right hand touched the stool, and a newspaper rustled, upon which bits of bacon and an empty liquor glass had been left the night before.

Gleb lazily watched as the room filled with light and took shape.

As if on photographic paper in a bath with a developer... Where is the negative then? he thought, and, as if intending to find out, hastily got up and walked in his underwear to the open window.

The sun's rays penetrated into the courtyard through a narrow passage between the apartment buildings and flickered in the crown of a poplar.

Almost half a century ago, when Gleb's parents moved into this newly built apartment building, someone stuck a freshly broken twig in front of the house. The young twig began to grow and turned into a tree.

"It would have been better if they had planted an apple tree," Gleb's mother once said. Neighbors, whose windows were facing the yard, sometimes complained that the poplar was blocking the sunlight. Yet no one cut it down.

A Zorki camera, a gift from his father, lay on the wide windowsill. Gleb stroked the leather case, frayed along the edges. He carefully unbuttoned it and smoothly pulled the lens out of the camera. The focus was set to infinity.

Just what I need, thought Gleb and cocked the camera shutter. He stepped over the threshold onto the balcony and looked into the viewfinder, into the distance — at an empty bench near an entryway. The shutter clicked.

"So that I can remember it," explained Gleb out loud although there was no one around.

He returned to the room, where boxes of books sat everywhere, and stood in the doorway. On the door frame, under a layer of white paint, he could barely see the pencil marks of his height made when he was a child. The lowest one was at his current waist level.

The walls in the bedroom were bare, and only Dostoevsky's portrait gleamed with a violet gloss in the corner. There used to be a desk by the window, at which Gleb would sit for several hours a day during his school years doing his homework or sawing something out with a jigsaw. His parents did not allow the door to be closed completely, and sometimes they peeped through the crack: "Glebushka is studying..." He tried to ignore it, but he felt humiliated and ashamed as if caught while performing a sinful act.

The old metal cot had been removed a long time ago; only a ginger suitcase and a box with the photographic enlarger stood at the entrance to the storage room, which the family usually called "*the dark room*".

Gleb remembered how once his father invited him in there, tightly shut the door and turned on a red light. He then showed Gleb the entire process of photo developing, step by step. Everything was effortless and simple, but in this simplicity, Gleb felt the genius of the inventor. His father scrolled through the film, and a series of silhouettes flashed inside a red square, difficult to define with an untrained eye. Finally, he chose the desired frame, put the light-sensitive paper under the magnifier and quickly pulled the shutter with his right hand.

"One, two, three, four..." his father whispered, making small movements with his left wrist, darkening the brightest parts of the picture, as if he were casting a spell. Then the exposed paper was put in the tub, and after a few seconds, familiar facial features of Gleb's mother appeared through the scarlet ripples of the developer liquid...

Tomorrow I'll give the enlarger to Peter; he collects such things, thought Gleb and bent over the ginger suitcase. *Why did my fa-*

ther never lock it? Things could have been so different!

Gleb finally found the key inside the suitcase and checked the locks.

Many years ago, when he was a teenager, Gleb climbed up the storage room shelves and removed this suitcase from the very top. His parents were not home, so the boy began to investigate the contents. Throwing back the lid of the suitcase, he found his father's army photographs, developed negatives, a developing tank and chemicals, and several certificates for innovation proposals... Gleb took out a stack of photographs from a yellowing envelope, and suddenly a small photograph fell out. It was of his much younger father. He was reclining, nude, in the shade of a squat tree, and his right elbow was buried in the grass. A tree branch hung, bent over him, and through the leaves, the rays of sunshine illuminated his face. Smiling, he looked straight at the camera. There was a date on the back of the photo: the picture was taken a year before Gleb's birth.

The teenage Gleb held the photo in bewilderment, not knowing what to do next. The

bright gaze and the laughing face of his naked father were disgusting to him. He realized that he could not just put the photo back and pretend that nothing had happened. He folded the picture in half and tore it with his trembling fingers. He tore each fragment into smaller and smaller pieces, until his fingers could barely hold the tiniest piece. He threw everything into a small trash can and, in slippered feet, carried it out into the courtyard. Holding his breath, he dumped the trash into the garbage container in the corner.

Gleb recalled that day many times. It was a mistake to destroy that photo, and he could not forgive himself.

Soon Gleb noticed that his father began to feel and look worse, and not only on the outside. Once they were riding a packed full tram, and he taught his son how not to give up your seat—you just had to stare out the window or pretend to be dozing.

The following year, his father suffered a stroke. Gleb's mother used all her connections to get her husband into a good clinic, but a week later, his physician refused to care for him further, and the disabled man was transferred to a psychiatric hospital outside the city.

Gleb brought him food on visiting days.

His father was squatting on the hospital bed, and the crumpled sheets did not hide his nakedness.

"How old am I?" he asked.

"Fifty-six," Gleb answered and handed him a quart-sized mason jar with buckwheat porridge.

"Fifty-six?" his father chuckled, curling his lips, and eagerly began shoveling the buckwheat into his mouth with a spoon.

A young female nurse scurried about between the beds, looking embarrased.

Several months passed. Gleb became withdrawn and avoided seeing his friends.

And then the hospital called to say that his father had passed away.

Four men carried the coffin down the stairs and placed it on two shabby stools under the concrete canopy of the entrance.

The goodbyes were said. The coffin was lifted onto the mournful shoulders and, accompanied by the music of the funeral march, was carried past the gray houses through the courtyard where the lone poplar tree was dropping its last leaves. In the brass band, Gleb's classmate Peter played a large trumpet. He played well.

"What if that photo was like a portrait of Dorian Gray? It's the most terrible thing ever! I killed my father!" Gleb reproached himself more than once.

After the funeral, a friend of the deceased asked Gleb to go to a place and deliver the sad news.

Climbing the wooden steps to the first floor of Maryana's house — that was the person's name — Gleb wondered why he was always chosen for such strange errands.

A beautiful elderly woman with sad eyes opened the door. Stepping inside, he found himself on a knitted rug, exactly like his grandmother had in the countryside village. A large mirror was hanging in the hallway, widening the space.

Gleb did not go farther in; he leaned against the doorframe. He noticed a photograph on the dresser: a young woman in a summer dress on a riverbank, with an airy cloud of fog above the water. He had seen this picture before — at home, in that ginger suitcase.

Gleb briefly told her about the death of his father. Maryana covered her face with her hands and turned away to face the window. Then through tears he heard her say, "She drove him to his death... nagged him to death..."

Gleb stood quietly, then muttered: "Excuse me, I have to go," and closed the door behind him.

Maryana was left standing by the window, looking out into the garden covered in the first snow of the season. An apple tree grew directly in front of the window. Its leaves had already fallen, but small red apples still clung to the top.

Maryana remembered the morning Platon invited her to accompany him to the countryside. From the bus terminus, they walked along the edge of the forest. The spicy scent of freshly cut grass wafted from a nearby field. The path went down to

a meadow and a river. By the river, next to a few willows, they found an old boat. Maryana took off her light shoes, set them on the wooden boardwalk and, holding the hem of her dress, stepped into the water. Fog was drifting over the river.

This can be an excellent shot! Platon felt excited and pulled out his Zorki camera he almost always carried with him. The shutter clicked. Platon lowered himself on his right knee and took another picture of Maryana.

A snag floated down the rapids, whirled in a whirlpool, and brushed against a sunken currant bush; the affected branch of the bush straightened quickly, and the driftwood moved on.

"Look!" Maryana exclaimed and then sighed and said: "That's how it happens in life too."

"Yes, it's impossible to photograph everything," said Platon, non-sequitur, and hung the camera on the oarlock.

He undressed, put his clothes on the side of the boat, then ran and front-flipped off the boardwalk into the river. Maryana watched with love in her eyes as he confidently swam towards the backwater. On a whim, she too took her clothes off in a thicket of willows and entered the river.

On the other bank, she wondered if Platon was much taller than her. They stood back-to-back, then turned to face each other.

"Come to my place," he said.

She agreed.

Maryana lit a candle.

Late into the night, one could see the silhouette of a woman in the semi-darkness of the window.

Gleb left Maryana's house and headed for the tram stop. It had stopped snowing and stars were twinkling high above. He jumped on the tram step, bought a ticket, and, clutching the cold steel handrails, rested his forehead against the wide window at the back of the car.

While listening to the steady knocking of the wheels, he wondered: *If back then Maryana had gotten pregnant by Platon, my father, I would not have been born at all. Many events would have been different. Another person would have been born, but it would not have been me. Not me! It turns out that I should be grateful to her as much as to my mother for my birth.* His head hurt.

Several stops early, Gleb jumped out of the tram and walked down the snow-covered street.

Such thoughts would not have come to me if I had lived these years differently, he thought. *And if I love myself (and I do!), then everything's fine. There were no mistakes! Why do I blame myself? The true cause of my father's illness could have been something else. After all, he deeply agonized about the collapse of the USSR, of the Communist Party, of the factory where he had worked all his life. And he drank heavily in recent years.*

Gleb calmed down and breathed in the air of the approaching winter. An empty tram rushed past with a screech. It was already dark when Gleb got home.

His mother greeted him.

Years passed. Gleb graduated from the Department of Mathematics, defended his Ph.D. thesis, and moved to the Netherlands for work. Once a year he came to his hometown and visited his mother. During these visits, he sometimes got together with friends, and they reminisced about their childhood.

One winter, COVID raged in the city. Gleb's mother did not avoid it. She was already in critical condition when she was put on a ventilator, and a week later she died. Due to the quarantine restrictions, Gleb was unable to attend her funeral. Six months later, he decided to sell the apartment. He threw almost all the furniture into a landfill. He donated the books to the city library and gave the enlarger to Peter in exchange for developing the last roll of film and printing the pictures. Some errands kept him in the city, so he moved to a hotel.

On his last day in Russia Gleb considered, *Should I pay Maryana a visit?*

He rejected the impulse, *What am I going to say? Maybe she still hates my mother. Even though I would like to, I can't ask her if she took that picture of my father...*

On that Sunday evening, Gleb met with Max, a friend and neighbor. They sat in a cozy coffee shop in the Zavodskoy district,[18] where only a brick chimney remained of the old factory. Gleb pulled several black-and-white photographs out of his pocket.

"Are you still into photography?" Max was surprised.

Gleb nodded.

"Do you remember making out with Natasha right here on this bench?" said Gleb and held out the picture.

---

[18] Factory district in Russian.

"I do! I liked her when I was younger, before I realized that she was ugly," said Max.

"And the bench... now it's a rarity," continued Max. "These benches next door were all destroyed."

Gleb's mobile phone rang.

"Yes, we're still on! As agreed... I'll be there!.. Of course," he answered and turned to Max, "Sorry, pal, I have to run."

Gleb took his stylish jacket off the back of the chair and held out his hand in a farewell handshake.

The next morning, the new owner of the apartment next door rang Max's doorbell.

"Your friend left it behind. I found it on a shelf in the storage room," he said and handed Max the portrait of Dostoevsky. "I don't know what to do with it."

After brushing the dust off the portrait, Max hung it in his kitchen on a nail in the wall: now he would have someone to have a cup of tea with!

Then he said out loud even though there was no one else in the room, "We'll live with integrity. Yes, sir!" He was so touched and so in character that he almost crossed himself, as if in front of a holy icon.

Meanwhile, Gleb had already landed in Amsterdam and successfully gone through the passport control.

The antediluvian ginger suitcase moved slowly on the baggage carousel.

Second Rescue

Here is the most important thing:
anyone can do it.
All it takes is closing one's eyes.[19]

Louis-Ferdinand Céline

From the Publisher
There are countless messages thrown into the sea from ships in distress: just think, for example, of Edgar Allan Poe. In the past, when someone found a message in a bottle sealed with wax, they would make an effort to help. However, if a message in the shape of a manuscript was found in a basement, it followed that help came either too late or was no longer needed since the author was safely rescued. We recently found such a manuscript. A young man, who served as a volunteer clearing the rubble after airstrikes in Ukraine, brought it to us. He insisted that he had found the notebook in the basement of a half-destroyed school. We were guided by a purely literary obsession when we decided to publish these notes without revealing the name of the author. After all, the war is not over yet.

A small plane flew high in the sky. A cloud of confetti fell out of it, shimmering in the sun. We stopped playing with the ball and watched with fascination as the cloud grew in size. A minute later, yellow leaflets fluttered between the five-story buildings in zigzags, down to the ground.

---

[19] A quote from the novel *Journey to the End of the Night* (1932) by Louis-Ferdinand Céline, a French novelist.

Andreika,[20] a red-haired boy from the building next door, who was 10 just like me, stood a little ways away. When the first leaflet touched the ground, he picked it up and shouted, "War!"

I shrank inside, *What is going to happen now?*

Zhenya, my older friend, grimly pushed out his lower lip and took a swing at the red-haired boy. Andreika crouched, shielded his face with his elbow and whined, "Don't! I was just kidding!" Zhenya wrestled the leaflet away from him; it turned out to be a "Best Wishes on Youth Day" message.

This memory of my happy childhood was my first clear thought once I recovered from the shellshock. That day, two cruise missiles had landed in the area of the town where I was found later. I had no idea how long I was unconscious. When I awoke, my near-sighted eyes made out a ruined wall of a house and a jagged section of a room with overturned furniture, all behind a wavering smoky haze. Something was burning; I smelled smoke...

What's happening? How... How did I get here? I thought, struggling to turn my head. It was as if everything around me was in a fog. I tried to yell, but I couldn't make a single sound. Reflexively, I reached out to push my glasses up on my nose, but they were missing.

Vague shadowy figures floated in the distance over a pile of rubble and twisted rebar. They came closer and turned into two tall men in camouflage

---

[20] Andreika is a nickname for male name Andrey.

fatigues. They loaded me into a wheelbarrow and took me down the deserted street to the nearest shelter, a back room of a shopping mall. A man in goggles and huge protective gloves was doing welding there: he was putting together Czech hedgehogs. The smell of carbide, familiar since childhood, brought me all the way back to reality.

I examined myself. My shirt was torn on my chest; I had small cuts and fresh scabs on my hands; several small shards of glass were stuck in my forearm. *Are these fragments of the hallway mirror?* I thought, trying to recall the moments before the catastrophe.

I remembered hearing an air-raid siren. Panicking, I rushed into the gloomy hallway: it was the safest place in my apartment. I turned on the light and did not recognize myself in the mirror: wide eyes stared at me through crooked glasses.

Why am I alone now? Will I die here? Alone? Inconceivable! These thoughts ran through my head.

I was not a believer and never prayed. Nevertheless, my life could end at any moment, and nothing would be left behind after me... My legs were shaking. A shot of vodka would be nice. There was a box of "Kyiv Vechirniy"[21] chocolates on the mirror stand. I couldn't remember anything else. Where did the chocolate come from? What happened a week ago, a month ago? All I remembered was a loud boom, then the reflection of the wall collapsed behind me, and the whole world went down with it. I was transported to hell in a split second...

Because of the blast injury, I could not move my legs. At first, I couldn't even speak, but that had already happened

---

[21] *Kyiv Vechirniy* is translated as "Late-Night Kyiv".

to me once before, when, as a child, I fell off a swing onto my back.

The next day I was able to stand, but still my feet did not fully obey me; my back ached badly. In the morning, the sirens went off again. Supported by some folks, I managed to move from the shopping mall shelter to a school basement. I refused medical aid by announcing that I was a physician myself, and that all I needed to get better was time.

Cots were built under the heating pipe wrapped in fiberglass. Women with children and some elderly people crouched on them, as well as on chairs and boxes here and there. I was directed to a vacant seat; somebody wrapped my shoulders in a knitted blanket. On the cot, I found a neat pile: a thick Algebra notebook and several textbooks, a gel pen, a sharpened pencil... I was told that a woman and her daughter had occupied the cot a couple of days earlier, but shortly before the new attack they had managed to escape town. They took only their most important possessions. The girl, a high school student, emptied her backpack of school supplies and put her cat into it. I read the name on the notebook cover: *Olena Prikhodko.* I had heard this name somewhere before, but where? Half of the notebook was filled with math problems and formulas. *Life can no longer be started from a clean slate... I will write down here everything that I can remember, and then my memory of the recent events will recover faster. So will the plan of my life, too,* I thought. At the same time I intended to refresh my school cursive writing lessons! Line up — inhale; line down — exhale. I focused on my breathing to clear my mind. I began to write on the graph paper, unwinding the **thread** that had tied my heart to this country.

The air-raid siren kept wailing, and soon many people crowded into the school basement. A young woman brought food in metal containers. Due to my nearsightedness, I could not see her well, but I imagined that this girl should have kind eyes and a gentle profile. She poured a hot drink into mugs. "Thank you, honey! I'm much warmer now!" said an old lady next to me.

After drinking the *uzvar*[22] I dozed off, remembering my trip to Kyiv with my ninth grade classmates during a long-ago winter break.

There was a crowd of parents; the hustle and bustle on the platform of the train station; my mother waving her hand. She had such a concerned expression on her face, as if I was going in the wrong direction. All of this happened a long time ago. The train was gaining speed. In the wake of the commotion at the station, the passengers of our third-class sleeper settled down. After checking and collecting the tickets, the conductor handed out clean-smelling sets of bed linens. I laid on the bottom berth, sometimes peeping out from under a thin woolen blanket and listening to the clacking of the wheels. Stripes of the sunset light flickered through the transparent curtains. Through the chug-chug of the wheels, one could hear the rattle of an empty glass in a glass-holder, as a reminder of the recent tea time. Sunset turned imperceptibly into night. Andrey, my classmate and friend, slept on the top berth. Suddenly the brakes screeched, and the train stopped. A fast train rushed past in the opposite direction with a long whistle.

On the second day of the trip, I got Leo Tolstoy's *War and Peace* out of my suitcase. I wanted to experience the moment when nothing exists in the world except for the immersion into a book. But reading was possible only occasionally; most of the time we played cards, told jokes, and played word chain games. All the while, the wheels kept on chugging at the junctions. We shared food. My mom gave me egg pies for the journey. At times, I did open the book but couldn't progress beyond the first page.

We sneaked out to smoke, pretending to go to the loo. Andrey was showing off; he smoked in the vestibule, occasionally spitting through the ajar gangway door open to the underside of the car, from whence came an icy draft. "How much longer to Kyiv?" he grumbled, conceitedly smoothing down his red curls. I silently looked out the sooty, narrow window. We paced

---

[22] *Uzvar* is a type of compote drink.

the long narrow aisle of the railcar back and forth; there was a stop schedule on the wall at the front, next to the hot water heater. The names of the stations were familiar to me from my *first* trip to Luhansk.

It was summer. I traveled with my grandmother and uncle. Green woods rolled by outside the window of our compartment, and the Ural Mountains rose ahead. My uncle, in an unbuttoned fatigue blouse, went out into the aisle and lowered the heavy window frame with both hands. Envious, I watched him, a six-foot tall man, pop his head out of the window and squint his tipsy eyes against the wind, puffing out cigarette smoke and making train sounds, to my delight: choo-choo-choo-oo... I left his birthday present — a toy locomotive with cars and a rail track — back home. The track could be put together in the shape of a circle or a figure eight, and the toy train would go on a loop until its spring unwound. I watched through the window as our train twisted and went into a tunnel... Unfortunately, before my departure, my mother dug all of my really important stuff out of my suitcase. There were pocket crossbows with arrows made from steel gypsy needles, a slingshot, and a toy pistol. What was I going to play with my cousins? Sandcastles?

A few years later, I found out that at the time, my uncle was reassigned from our Siberian Military district to the Luhansk Military Navigator School. *He could have told me a lot of interesting things about the ratings of fighter aircraft*, I thought, standing in the cold vestibule.

Meanwhile, Andrey explained to me the structure of battleships and torpedo boats... "I want to go to the Naval Academy after school," he suddenly shared his most sacred desire. "The sea has so many opportunities for adventure! Will you come with me?"

I was astonished by the question for a minute, and then exhaled, "Come on, no way!" Still, I was flattered to receive such an invitation from my friend.

We were on the road for four days: it was thousands of miles to Ukraine!

I remember only one tour of Kyiv, out of all of them; it was to a dungeon. There were relics in a niche under a heavy canopy: a skull and skeletal remains. Anxious, I looked around, searching for my classmates and the teacher, who was my homeroom and Algebra teacher.

Suddenly, I realize that I am not in the Kyiv-Pechersk Lavra dungeon, but in a dim school basement, and there is no way out because of the ceaseless air raids.

Electricity is off. Candles flicker, iPhone screens give some light, as do the blue cones of flashlights. Someone brought a kerosene lamp. Some people around me have lost their relatives, their homes... Words in Ukrainian and Russian are heard from everywhere in the basement, and humor, sorrow, hate, bitterness, and love are all intertwined:

"F**king Russians!"

"We can try to make it to the store and get some tea to brew."

"After a few hours, the old lady will be asking: is it the ninth or tenth siren?"

"I have had anxiety for a long time, for many months, no, not months, years, actually!"

"This is crazy! Are they all mad over there? Bitches! Enough of this!"

An elderly man mutters, "The question has been raised; the question has been raised. This is what the desire to unite the lands can lead to..."

A young woman is telling the events of the past day, "I was doing some laundry. I took a wash-basin with wet clothes and went to the balcony. I heard a rumble, as if a jet plane was flying: whirr! I barely turned my head before a two-story long winged missile flew out as if from behind my shoulder and slammed into the opposite building. And there must be just a hundred yards to it, my balcony faced that building. Still can't get this image out of my mind... The blast wave was not very strong. People said that the missile did not explode, and it was removed from the building afterwards. Still, a few apartments were destroyed."

A woman with straggly hair sings a Ukrainian lullaby to a child, "*Goyda, goyda-goy, night has come to us. It's time for the little kids to sleep...*"

It turns out that I can understand some Ukrainian, but I cannot speak it.

"The war has started because of people like him," a muffled and hoarse voice is heard, aimed at me. The others start to shush the speaker...

My ID card, iPhone, and glasses are lying somewhere nearby under the ruins of a five-story building... *So, I am completely reset to zero*, I think, trying to remember the address of that apartment.

Initially, they did not notice me or ignored me. People were busy thinking about their own concerns, which I could not understand at first. Most came only during the air-raid sirens. Those who lost their homes stayed at the shelter, waiting for a chance to hitch a ride out of town. Since I was deeply aware of the inappropriateness of my being here, I lay under the blanket, curled in a Z, on the wooden cot. My identity separated from me, hanging from that pipe in the gloom, thinking about whether to return or not.

I haven't felt so unwelcome and useless in a long time...

On the way back from that trip to Kyiv with my classmates, I spent three days at the Kazansky railway station in Moscow. The eastbound rail traffic was at a halt: there were snow drifts on the tracks in the Ural region. The travel allowance from our parents was spent quickly. We drank boiling water, like Chuck and Gheck.[23]

At last, the rail tracks were cleared. Holding on to the cold gangway handrails, we climbed up the icy steps into the vestibule of the sleeping car. The overcrowded third-class sleeper was well heated, and this created a feeling of reliability and comfort. Our homeroom teacher assured the conductor that

[23] Characters from the story *Chuck and Gheck* by Arkady P. Gaidar, a Russian Soviet writer.

she would pay for our meals upon arrival. So food was brought to us from the dining car in small metal pots. This was an incredible bliss after starving for days at the railway station in Moscow!

Clara, a girl with large black eyes, leaned on the table and squinted at the window, where the endless snow-covered fields flashed by. It was getting dark. I sat opposite in a side seat, watching her in the reflection of tinted glass. We hadn't known each other before this trip. It turned out that Clara was from Kyiv. Her mother traveled with us as a chaperone. For the past three years, they had lived in my neighborhood, and Clara was a year behind me at school.

One January evening, a few days after returning from the trip, Clara called me and asked for help with Algebra homework. My sheepskin coat unbuttoned, holding the flaps tightly with one hand, I crossed the yard on a narrow path between grayish snowdrifts, past the snow-covered poplars where a wooden swing had hung as recently as last summer.

The math problems turned out to be easy, but Clara could not understand the algorithm of the solution, no matter how hard I struggled to explain it. I began to visit her place quite often, driven by the desire to help. Sometimes her friend Nelya came to see Clara. One day, Clara took a film-strip projector out of the closet and, focusing the beam of the projector on a whitewashed wall, suggested we watch some old stories on slides. I remember the one about Pan Niteczka.[24] Fancy that: he had such a narrow throat that he could eat only noodles! "He doesn't have any teeth, does he?" I doubted. Nelya laughed; Clara said that it was a make-believe, and I had no imagination.

She lived with her mother. Whatever happened to her father, I never asked. Clara's mother was nice. Serving us small pies, she enthusiastically talked about horoscopes and how one's fate could be explained by the intricate movement of the plan-

---

[24] Pan Niteczka is a character of a book written by Kornel Maku-szyński, a Polish writer of children's and youth literature.

ets. I fell into deep contemplation; but, after looking at the problem from another side, I soon enrolled into an astronomy club. Nelya also began attending the meetings. The lecturer once said that the Tunguska meteorite fell at the same latitude as Leningrad, and if the catastrophe had occurred a few hours later, then the driving force of Russian history would have gone in a completely different direction. *How can we believe in horoscopes after that?* I thought.

In August, our club traveled outside the city to a river bank to observe the Perseids meteor shower. Clara joined us. It was a warm night. We lay motionlessly in an open meadow in sleeping bags with our heads to the north and looked into the dark abyss. Stars fell from time to time. We heard joyful, jubilant exclamations: "There is one!" or "Not bad at all over there!" And someone's hand soared upwards. We had to determine the direction of each meteor and mark its vector on the star chart, in order to later find the radiant at the intersection of the lines.

I liked Clara. She had black hair with straight bangs. In the morning, she stepped lightly along the sandbar and sang in a pretty voice, "I so want the summer to last forever..."[25] A long log, polished by waves, lay on the bank. Clara stepped onto it, and I offered her my hand in assistance.

"Did you make a wish when the stars were falling?" she asked, balancing with her whole body.

"I don't believe in that," I replied timidly.

"But I made one," she said mysteriously, moving her hips, and after taking a few more smooth steps, she deftly jumped to the ground.

I was still holding her cool hand. Hand in hand, we walked further along the sandbar towards a dense pine forest, and then together we stepped onto a path covered with pine needles. Sometimes the path leaped onto a high bank, where the wide river splashed below in the rays of the sun, exposing countless pebbles. We stopped at one of the pines above

---

[25] A quote from the song *Starry Summer*, performed by Alla Pugacheva, a famous Soviet singer, in 1980.

a steep cliff. Clara leaned against the trunk to remove the pine needle that was poking her in the foot. I came closer and, seeing her dark eyes so close, hesitated. Then I carefully pressed my lips against hers in a first kiss. We returned to the camp feeling a little bit woozy, and smiling with swollen lips.

"Where did you go? The bus to the city has been waiting for a long time!" Nelya called out to us when we came out onto the sandbar again.

It felt like fall was approaching. In the late summer, Clara and her mother left for Kyiv. As it turned out later, she never came back. I was a little sad, but I still could not understand whether I was in love with her.

The following year, I entered the university to study medicine and soon forgot about Clara. Predicting the birth and death of stars was rather tempting, but I chose medicine out of all the sciences.

The damp basement air becomes heavier at night. Sometimes I just space out and can't figure out if I'm dreaming or if it's a deception of perception. But I persistently continue to glean visual images from the past; mechanically, I record them on paper. I do so carefully, bending my finger, thereby increasing the value of each word. Perhaps, I will finally reach the present time via the emotional struggles of the past and understand what is happening around me. I have never thought that I would be recalling my early years as events that are important to me. I remember some details vividly, and it is funny, because how can they matter now? Although... Who knows? Maybe by collecting more of these memories, I will be rescued.

"But if I describe everything in detail, then I will need a whole 'nother life," I say this thought aloud.

"That's good! You will have something to do," my female neighbor replies with a smile: a woman in a headscarf with small wrinkles on her face, just like my grandmother from my distant childhood. She is knitting a sweater, moving steel needles slowly. There is a small icon of the Virgin Mary on the suitcase in front of her. The woman smiles one more time, awkwardly, puts aside her knitting and pulls a photograph out of her bag, proudly saying, "And this is my son, he serves in the Ukrainian Armed Forces!"

During the internship, I enrolled as a lab assistant on the *Zdorovie*,[26] a floating boat clinic. I measured blood pressure, drew blood, and recorded electrocardiograms. Natasha, ten years older than me, was the physician. Every time I put electrodes on the chest of a young female patient, Natasha blushed. I had always dreamed of great love like in novels, but natural instincts won, and our relationship progressed on the fifth day of our journey to the north. In the evenings — there was a polar twilight all night long at these latitudes — after landing in some abandoned village, where there was not even a pier, we went down the steep gangway to the shore and walked away from the ship for a hundred yards, holding hands, and embraced by unquenchable light, and walked along the wet pebble beach.

At night, I sneaked into her tiny cabin, where a small glass porthole reminded me of outer space where stars were born and died, while we held each other. Her eyes closed, Natasha moaned softly in my arms, her eyelashes fluttering. At that moment I felt like I was flying, while she whispered, "You will remember me... you will..." But every time after that she sent me off, explaining that she did not want to get attached to me. "See you tomorrow, Gulliverov," she said with a smile, mocking my last name. I turned around at the doorstep and watched her huddle under the covers about to fall asleep.

Sometimes Natasha brought novels by George Sand or Wilkie Collins out of her travel bag; these were the books that my mother liked to read. But I breathed a sigh of relief when the boat moored at my native river port after

---

[26] *Zdorovie* is translated to English as "health".

three months of sailing in the Siberian latitudes. *Land! the sailors shouted. Land!* I recited in my head, walking down the creaking gangway with a suitcase in my hand. A man was waiting for Natasha at the landing. Her husband? She accepted the bouquet and buried her face in the flowers. I seized the opportunity and brushed by, sneaking off into the crowd...

The thought of finding my destiny would not leave me be; therefore, as soon as I graduated from the university, I first passed an interview with *an important government agency*, where Andrey worked, and then I accepted a job as a physician on a large ship. How else could I combine my wanderlust with work? I had to mature; people say that traveling contributes to that. Besides, there are fewer temptations on a ship... "We will let you know when we need you," I was told at the KGB office. I wondered what they would expect from me, as I descended the marble staircase flanked by columns.

I visited almost every continent. I sent postcards and some-times a detailed letter from every new country to my mother. She loved reading my handwritten messages so much! In the evenings, I went out on the deck, looking at the night sky and searching for the Southern Cross. Walking along the many-voiced coastal paths, where the splash of sea waves can be heard, I met African girls. I can't recall other details of those wander-ings; you should really read the novel by Johnathan Swift about the adventures of a ship's physician Lemuel Gulliver. I do re-member Ukraine: Sevastopol, Odesa...

And then one day, the Soviet Union collapsed, and I ended up in Ukraine: a different country, but also my home.

One day I found myself in the evening capital and was walk-ing along Bankovaya Street, feeling unloved. By the House with Chimaeras, I realized that I had been here in my youth, with my classmates. A historical site! Still as if in a dream, I politely asked a young lady how to get to the subway and heard a fa-miliar voice respond. It was Clara! How was this possible? She gasped in surprise; it took her a bit to recognize me, "Verov? Yegor! I can't believe my eyes! Look at you, a grown man!" We started talking. Clara had already been married and had a new last name, Prikhodko... The notebook I am writing in now is signed by this name. Is there any connection? Or is it just a co-incidence?

The next day we met in a cafe on Khreshchatyk and ordered chocolate croissants. Clara told me how nine years previous-ly — it's amazing how time flies! — she happened to be in my city. Her father was assigned to the Siberian military district. But he was rarely home. Soon they learned that he had an affair with another woman. Her mom filed for divorce, and they returned to Kyiv. Clara did not want to go and was close to committing suicide in a state of depression... It was obvious that she was struggling while telling this story.

"And how are you doing?" she asked. In response, I started to talk about my travels, telling — and embellishing — some stories about the storm, how we rescued Chinese fishermen, about whales and cold icebergs.

We looked at each other with fascinated eyes. She was still attractive... *How could I have never thought about her in all these years?* I thought.

That's how I decided to quit the sea and stay on land.

(A page was torn out here.)

Working for a pharmaceutical company, I sold medicinal leeches and traveled all over Ukraine. I often visited my aunt in Luhansk. She was already in her late 60s, but she never complained. In her youth, she was fascinated by servicemen, and after her husband passed, she had a colonel as her life partner. But she outlived him, too. In the cozy room where I usually spent the night, his uniform overcoat with epaulets and stripes hung in the closet.

Life with her was easy: she did not bother me with tedious conversations about not walking in the dark, not sitting where it's drafty, or not dressing warmly enough. We went out on the balcony, ate sweet cherries, and drank tea. I confessed that when I was a child and visited them with my grandmother in Luhansk, I ran with her sons around the neighborhood in the evenings, and cut down clotheslines to play lasso with. Then I taught my cousins how to make crossbows and toy pistols... I recalled how I almost got lost on the way to Luhansk, while having a bout of somnambulism. I walked after a man who looked like my aunt's husband and went to another station via a connecting passage. There, my head finally cleared, and I found myself among strangers. On the way back home, my mother did not come to pick us up; instead of the Kharkov train, confused, she waited for the speed train from Khabarovsk. The country was so huge that geography did not fit into the memory of ordinary people... My aunt silently nodded, playing a complex game of solitaire; then she became sad because her sons had gone to a better world by that time.

I began to tell my aunt that my return to my homeland was out of the question. Feeling angry, I spat cherry pits on the green lawn and thought that I was happy here because Clara, my Clara, lived in a nearby town.

A few days after my fortunate rescue, I started to walk confidently. Once, feeling bored, I went into the hallway and began to explore the basement. It turned out that there was another room next door, and the lock on the door was broken. I peered inside, illuminating the space with my flashlight; it was a military museum devoted to an army division. Artifacts, imbued with the fighting spirit, faced me from the stands covered with cobwebs and dust, snatched out of the darkness by the light. Among them were half-decayed military IDs, rusty rifles, green shell casings, a boatswain's whistle... I staggered backwards when I saw my face, covered with stubble, as if that of a stranger, in the tinted glass of the next artifact's case. There were rusty surgical instruments from a field hospital on the stand. Medical instruments! I recalled that once and only once I had to operate urgently to remove an infected appendix of one of the passengers when I was a ship's physician. In the middle of the operation, my hands started to shake, and cold sweat ran down into my eyes. It was only thanks to the experience and self-control of the assisting nurse that everything ended well. Suddenly, somewhere upstairs, there is a loud crash, the glass of the museum displays trembles, and I hurry back to my shelter.

It's been more than three weeks since I showed up in the basement. Is there any higher meaning to this? During these weeks, I have reached a state of almost complete mindlessness and insensibility. Memories lost their cohesion. Meditation through calligraphy does not help. I doze off repeatedly.

It was getting dark when Nikolai and Stepan, my neighbors in the shelter, and I went upstairs to prepare food. We looked around. Earlier that day, the scene further deteriorated: a part of the roof was demolished in the building opposite, other buildings stood with broken windows. The glow of a distant fire could be seen on the horizon: the city's power plant was burning. Nikolai was furious. "Can you imagine that '*arbiter of people's fates*' giving the order with a smirk?" he said in a low voice. "Or the bastard who calculates the trajectory of a death-dealing missile in the morning, and at night goes back to his lover."

In such circumstances, Stepan normally uses some revoltingly gross expletives, but this time he doesn't; he only grits his teeth angrily and spits on the ground with hate. I hang my head; I don't want to believe that people are capable of committing heinous crimes. There wouldn't be any sense in such a world. Something needs to be done. "If there were flower seedlings in these boxes," I nod towards the school greenhouses, "I would plant them in the flower beds."

Stepan and Nikolai look at each other. "You go too far," Nikolai says. "It's not so easy to do ordinary good things in the Stone Age reality." I agree internally; usually I'm easy to persuade.

Having broken down empty wood boxes with the smell of last year's earth into firewood, we light a fire. Stepan fetches potatoes, rice, and water. We cook a stew: we toss the ingredients in the water and put the pot on two bricks over the fire. A silence lasts for several minutes, except for the crackling of the fire. After a while, Stepan takes out a flask and pours vodka into mugs. We clink our mugs together: "Long live Ukraine!" Then we drink some more.

We seem to have talked about everything on Earth in the past couple of days, so, feral and unshaven, we fall silent and watch the dying flame. The last sparks shoot out of the campfire, soaring upwards. The city sleeps without electricity, and the stars are clearly visible in the sky. I recall my youth: maybe I can make a wish; why not? I am waiting for a meteor to fall, but, apparently, this is neither the time nor the place for it. Then I suddenly imagine that we have been shipwrecked and are on an *uninhabited* island. After fishing out the leftovers of food from the ocean, we find shelter in a cave and now hope to be rescued. There is no one around. Not a sound, not a rustle! We are frightened of this silence and uncertainty.

My daydream is shattered by the barking of abandoned dogs.

Yesterday, an evacuation vehicle came by early in the morning. I refused a seat in favor of a woman with a child and went out to see them off. A dusty sedan with a broken bumper and bullet holes in the trunk waited at the curb in the shade of a chestnut tree. Before the woman left, we walked to the next-door building where her mother had died under a concrete slab during a bombing a few days ago. She was buried in a bomb crater on the playground near the swings without a cross or tombstone. The woman burst into tears by the sandy mound of the grave and, glancing back at the ruins of the apartment building, she clutched a handkerchief in her fist and hurried with her daughter to the car. I rushed to the driver-guide to ask if I could get a job as a doctor on his team. He nodded and promised to pick me up on the next trip, then started the engine. I stared after them. The car picked up speed, raising a dust whirl. Chestnut trees and candle-shaped poplars grew high in the fog behind the square.

Last night there was an explosion on the surface, and a massive jolt ran through the vaulted ceiling. The exit from the basement filled up with rubble, while the wall separating our room from the school's military museum sagged a bit, and a narrow gap opened just above my cot. Before I leave, I will put my notes into this "portal" since I want to deliver them to other people. Although my notes are somewhat disjointed and contradictory, I did my best not to tire the future reader with excessive confessions.

I almost stopped writing, but not because of the lack of light: during daytime it seeps in through the windows, as narrow as log pillbox holes, right under the ceiling. In the evenings, the yellow kerosene lamp flickers dimly; it's more cheerful with it, despite the caustic fumes that sting inside my nose. Water drips from the pipe, tapping on the bottom of a bowl. It is strange because I would have been terribly annoyed by this tapping in a different time. Now it beats like a metronome, specific only to this environment. My soul tunes into this rhythm, slipping into oblivion...

Is everything around me just a product of my imagination?
Sometimes it seems that it is such an absurd idea to journal in this situation, even if the notes are copied three times over in beautiful handwriting! I am more concerned with other questions: How deeply am I involved in these tragic events? Have I followed someone in another bout of somnambulism? Will I be happy if I can recall everything? Could my life be pure nonsense? I hope that I never acted like a bastard, never did any nasty things, never humiliated anyone. Well, if I did someone wrong, and I'm guilty, then please forgive me!

We've run out of food. We are drinking rusty water from the pipe. The air is fetid and stuffy. My body does not obey me well, it is difficult to get up, my limbs go numb.
Sitting in the semi-darkness, I look through the first pages of the notebook. One system of equations with two unknown variables remains unsolved. At school, I solved such problems quite well. A thought came to my mind: *If I solve it, we will be rescued.*

There are now three of us left: Stepan, Nikolai, and myself. Yesterday, Vladimir Sergeevich, an older man who had occupied a cot in the far corner, had a heart attack. He breathed heavily, wheezing, and could barely speak. There were purple bruises on his cheeks. And I couldn't help! Today he became unresponsive. When I came up to him and touched his open chest, he was already cold. A blissful smile was frozen on his face, faintly visible in the dim light.

There was a growing murmur of voices outside. Nikolai warned us that phones and notes could be taken away. If there are any "information carriers", then it is better to hide them: put them in some hole or bury them. "Pretend that you haven't existed before," he advised.

Fear has left me. I become calm. *Whatever happens, happens!* I think.

There is a bright light. It hurts my eyes.

There is a voice.

"Get your IDs ready!"

In a moment, I will see my rescuers. Or executioners.

From the Publisher

We were curious to learn about the further fate of Yegor. It turned out that Clara and her daughter went to Poland via the immigration program for refugees. She did not answer our phone calls. We found Stepan and Nikolai, with whom he had hid in the basement; later, Yegor was also hospitalized with Stepan.

Stepan said that a man with an impassive face and receding reddish hair came into Yegor's ward once. It was obvious that they knew each other; they even hugged. Yegor called him Andrey. The man exclaimed, "Verov? You are alive! Well, brother, you were born lucky! Just wait, soon there will be legends about the miraculous rescue of the ship's physician!" The man wondered whether Yegor had been starving or freezing in the basement. Then he hinted that Yegor had been lazy for too long, and it was high time to repay his debt to the motherland. "We will give you a chance to smell gunpowder, the opportunity to be a hero! Tomorrow we go to Sevastopol! All aboard!" Andrey said it with an unctuous smile and, patting Yegor on the shoulder, handed him a draft notice. After, Yegor went out into the hallway, supposedly to the bathroom. He has not been seen after that. Two empty cups were left on his bedside table as a reminder of the recent tea time.

"Shortly before our rescue, Yegor casually mentioned that he decided to sign up as a doctor with the medical evacuation team," Nikolai told us over the phone. "Frankly, I was then doubtful of his words because it seemed to me that he was quite removed from the problems of our country. He was a strange, distant man. But, regardless, he is a doctor, he can save people. If he really decided to do that, then, most likely, he crossed over the front line. Well, a worthy act, a heroic one, even."

That may have been true. Not every person is able to illegally cross the front line: one must have courage, or at least an adventurous spirit, to do it. And after the crossing, to act sweet and play solitaire with an aunt in a peaceful home, lying with inspiration about his last, very short trip to the homeland, about the impending return to the big ship, and the future unlimited travels and wanderings around the world. And finally, in some far away tropical country, where there are neither guns nor tanks, he will come to a crossroads and without hesitation, seized by marvelous delight, follow one of the roads, no matter which one: there is beauty everywhere as far as the eye can see, and birds are singing.

Victoria's Secrets

The parking lot was a hundred yards from the orphanage, and visitors had to walk through a pine forest. Holding a large flat box under his arm, Roman walked along the path, covered with reddish pine needles, squinting into the sun from time to time. His face, as long as a fiddle, soon broadened into a gracious smile. On each visit to the orphanage, he felt that his life was meaningful, and that neither his own home nor work could matter so much.

Two years previously, his wife Maria got seriously ill, and surgery was needed to stop the internal bleeding and save her life. After the surgery, Maria became infertile. When she was discharged from hospital, she stayed in bed for a long time, staring at the ceiling, silent. "I am an empty vase, completely empty," she said one day, and, covering her face with her hands, turned it to the wall. A few months later she got stronger but did not allow any intercourse with her husband. Then, one day she made a hint that she would not mind if he went for a two-time.

"Stop saying that! I love only *you*! Everything will be okay. We will adopt a child from an orphanage," Roman encouraged her. But Maria straight out refused; she did not believe that it was possible to create a strong traditional family this way.

What is the reason to live? We don't have children; we don't have and won't have any future, thought Roman. Sometimes he could not stay home, seeing his wife in her depression. Maria was a beautiful woman. She was almost ten years younger than her husband, but after that surgery she faded somehow. Her facial features became sharper, and the difference in years disappeared. Roman realized that he could not bring joy to his wife anymore, only pain.

He began to leave home early and return late. He often spent his evenings in the company of his old pals, with whom he had drank to "our Crimea" seven years ago. They sat in restaurants with somebody else's wives, chatting about this and that. Late in February 2022, a new era began. "We should have done *it* then," his friends said. Roman nodded neutrally; he did not want to break the friendly harmony, since he believed that is what was necessary for their person-to-person interaction.

One day, wandering like a sleepwalker around his native City-on-the-River on a warm May evening, he thought: *I must leave something behind, imprint myself on memory...* He saw some artist sets in a shop-window on the central avenue: pencils, boxes of paints, and crayons. He remembered that he drew quite well in his youth; he even attended art school, from which, however, he never graduated. *Shall I try again?* Roman thought. He went into the shop and bought a set of pastel crayons and paper. The next day, he left the city for a plein-air painting early in the morning, while his wife was still sleeping.

Since then, Roman spent every weekend in nature: he walked along the forest edges and sketched. On a warm summer day, he was walking along the river bank, enjoying the beauty of the landscape, when he noticed a house on the top of a sloping hill, almost completely overgrown with forest. The two-story wooden mansion was barely visible between the trees, and only the high roof, decorated with intricately carved dragons, could be seen completely by an accidental passer-by. Choosing a suitable angle, Roman unfolded his chair and took out the crayons... He did not finish the sketch, so he decided to come here again.

Roman learned that the house was built in the Late Art Nouveau style more than a hundred years ago. In the middle of the 20th century, it was the summer residence of a high-ranking member of the Communist Party of the City Committee. During the reformation period, called Perestroika, there was enormous controversy about this building and finally, the new city authorities handed the mansion over to the orphanage called The Scarlet Sails.

The next day, Roman called the orphanage and offered his help. They were eager to accept.

At first, it was not easy. Adult world communication skills did not work here. Roman did not know how to talk with the children or how to act. The orphanage caregivers came to his rescue and gave advice. He spent almost a year caring for the orphaned children.

"Good morning, Anna Pa'l'na!" Roman said when he saw the orphanage Principal on the porch.

"Ah, Roman Lvovich! Hello, my dear! You haven't visited us for a long time," Anna Pavlovna replied, glancing at him over

her shoulder. She was trying to feed a squirrel out of her hand. Not daring to approach the human, the squirrel jumped on the branches of the nearest pine tree, balancing with its fluffy tail.

Roman stood at the door, watching that tranquil scene, and said:

"I feel so good in this place! Once I come here, my heart and soul can rest. There is amazing air! I inhale, and inhale, and can't breathe in enough!" And confirming his words, he deeply inhaled the tarry air of the pine forest.

Anna Pavlovna could not wait for the squirrel to finally descend from the tree anymore. She placed the nuts onto the wide porch railing. Roman opened the door for her. At the entrance he nodded to an elderly guard with a puffy face and angry eyebrows.

"Leave it in my office for now," Anna Pavlovna pointed to the cardboard box containing a Lego set, which Roman carefully held with both hands.

"We have new children. Two arrived yesterday from the liberated territories. Come on!"

And, deftly grabbing Roman's arm, she led him down the corridor.

They entered a large playroom, where several children of different ages sat at tables.

"These are Vicky[27] and Peter... Children, meet Roman Lvovich, our guardian and frequent visitor," Anna Pavlovna said in a high pleasant voice.

Peter, a slightly stooping bespectacled boy of about eleven, barely perceptibly nodded his head, looking up from the computer for only a second. Behind him, in the far corner of the room, a girl of about thirteen with huge hazel eyes and blond curly hair to her shoulders stood lost.

Roman knew every child by name. He called them up one by one to come to him and asked how things were going. He had not seen them for almost a month. He'd been to the capital on a business trip, representing his construction company, and

---

[27] Vicky is a short name for Victoria.

then there was a city council meeting and making acquaintance with the new governor. They had discussed the current project for the municipal bridge reconstruction.

Anna Pavlovna observed the interaction with silent sympathy. Soon she brought the new set of Lego out from the office. And when Roman was about to leave, she told him that the Cossacks would come next Saturday to give a lesson on patriotism. Roman knew he wouldn't be needed. *I will find something else to do,* he thought.

A week later, Roman went for a plein-air sketching with peace of mind. Five hundred yards before his usual turn, he turned onto a country road towards the river. Once out of the car, he found a spot from where he drew the orphanage building for the first time. It had been a year since he discovered it! Putting a cardboard box with a sheet of paper on his knees, he sketched out the composition of a future landscape: a winding path along a flowering spring meadow leading to a gentle wave-shaped hill, where the wonderful roof with dragons could be seen between the pines.

He was so passionate about drawing that he did not notice Vicky quietly approach him.

Roman didn't like it when someone looked over his shoulder, but this time the girl's gaze didn't bother him.

"I would like to be in your picture," Vicky said unexpectedly. She turned the visor of her baseball cap towards the back of her head. Her thin lips stretched into a smile.

"I'm not a magician," Roman answered jokingly and looked at Vicky attentively.

A flicker of mild laughter flashed in the girl's eyes.

"Let's go to the river! Do you want to?" she asked softly and, lowering her long eyelashes, went ahead without looking back.

Her words had a magical effect on him. He felt as if he had returned to his distant childhood. Roman put aside the crayons and forgot about his age, since he immediately turned into a boy, who was ready to fulfill any whims of a neighbor girl. Enchanted, he followed her. The path led to a shallow ravine with a gurgling brook. In this place overgrown with bushes, he held out his hand and exclaimed:

"Be careful! Step on the plank!"

Vicky took a step, but slipped and lightly brushed his chest for a moment, then laughed softly.

On the way, Roman talked to the girl about his youth: he loved drawing, so he went to the Academy of Architecture, and lately he had been working as an engineer in a construction company designing bridges. He could tell stories about bridges for hours! Vicky told him her own sad story: her mother drowned in the sea when she was six years old, and she did not remember her father. It took some time for Peter and her to reach this place. "He is not my brother. We lived in the same orphanage," Vicky explained.

At the steep bank, the path went down sharply, and it was dangerous to go down to the water. A large full-flowing river made a bight here and washed away the bank, churning water at the edge. The sound of falling stones could be heard repeatedly. Vicky looked intensely down, where the main stream sparkled in the sun rays.

"You have visitors today. Why did you run away?" Roman asked, breaking the silence.

"They didn't sing songs, only talked about soldiers. I got bored and left," the girl smiled awkwardly.

"Well, that is a convincing argument," Roman said, looking up at the darkened sky. Across the river, flashes of the approaching thunderstorm were visible. Then he began to explain what lightning was and why thunder was barely audible.

The wind blew harder, the tops of the trees swayed in unison. "Now, it's time to get back! And hurry up!" Roman said.

Without looking back, they hurried up the hill, as the first drops of rain pelted the hushed leaves. Roman said goodbye to the girl at the orphanage entrance and ran back. The rain picked up, and when he returned to his spot, he found the abandoned sketch completely soaked. The painted dragon on the roof ridge increased in size and turned into a fire-breathing one. *What a pity! But apparently, everything is God's will. No big deal, Monet also painted his haystacks many times. Next time I will do it even better, but this piece could not be restored, unless I do it from memory.* Roman was thinking out loud partly in jest and partly seriously, heading to the car.

Roman soon realized that he visited the orphanage because of Vicky. He brought her colored pencils and boxes of paints. He taught her how to draw. He felt that the orphanage staff expected him to adopt Vicky. Sometimes the thought of adoption came to his mind, but his wife did not want to foster an orphan. "Don't you see what time we live in? If I were younger and healthier, I would go work there as a nurse tech. Nobody knows what will happen tomorrow," she said.

Roman remembered Maria proudly marching on Victory Day[28] with a portrait of her great-grandmother, who worked in a hospital during WWII. It was just a year ago. And now there was no march of the Immortal Regiment.[29] "Well, it's good that they canceled it," Roman suggested. "It is no longer clear whether this is about that war or about this one."

---

[28] Victory Day is a holiday that commemorates the Soviet victory over Nazi Germany in 1945.

[29] The Immortal Regiment march is a civil memorial event in Russia during the Victory Day (May 9) celebrations.

In the center of the City-on-the-River, a huge letter **Z** hung on the facade of the Drama Theater. And a billboard on Pochtamskaya Street shouted: "Everything For the Front! Everything For the Victory!" If not for these signs, no one would know that something terrible was happening. The citizens did not want to discuss the war in Ukraine, even in their private circles in the kitchen. Some were afraid of being reported because there were show trials already. Others realized that telling the truth is difficult and comforted themselves with the words: "We don't know everything." Some people were sure that Europe would soon run out of money, China would help us, and we would win. No one wanted to think about defeat. To escape from unpleasant thoughts, they went to concerts. Many musicians and artists came to visit that year! Could we have ever imagined that there would be Gergiev's[30] tour in our city?

Roman was not a fan of classical music, but he could not refuse when his wife offered to go to the concert of the great conductor. *You can lie, steal, and still make people happy,* he thought after the performance.

Roman spent more and more time at the orphanage. Anna Pavlovna expressed her concern that Vicky was drawing a lot but never showed her work. She was constantly sad, stopped saying good morning, and answered "yes" or "no". And what secrets could a child have?

"And, you know, I think she believes you will adopt her!" the Principal whispered in the corridor, taking Roman by the elbow. "But keep in mind, Peter is basically her shadow! There they were in the same orphanage, although there are no documents proving that they are related."

In early summer, Roman started taking Vicky to the Art school.

"I dream of living in my own house with a workroom," Vicky once said on the way back and added: "My house has to sit next to the forest so that I may breathe freely."

---

[30] Valery A. Gergiev, a famous Russian conductor.

"You talk like a grown-up," Roman said in response.

A shadow suddenly flickered across the girl's face. She remembered the artillery and missile attacks and averted her eyes, glistening with tears. Roman felt that something was wrong. Turning into a quiet lane, he stopped the car and offered to go to a cafe.

"What will you have? An Éclair or ice cream?" Roman asked, as they sat down at the table.

Vicky thought for a second and immediately cheering up, she burst out:

"Both?!"

"Of course," Roman replied.

He watched her gobble up the chocolate cream and searched his mind for something he would ask now if he had been her father. Then, feeling generous, he had a crazy idea: *Maybe I shall bring her home to visit? After all, my wife is on vacation in Thailand; no complicated explanations will be needed.*

"I have albums with the Impressionists' works," Roman said as they entered his apartment.

"Impressionists? Who are they?" Vicky asked.

"Here is Monet, for example," Roman said, taking a heavy book from the shelf. "Take a look, while I go and cook something to eat." He wanted to treat her to some tasty homemade food.

Returning to the room half an hour later, he found Vicky on the sofa. The girl slept with her bare legs tucked under. She had put on his crimson shirt that half-covered her thin thighs. Her dress hung on the back of the chair. A *Victoria's Secret* catalog sat on the coffee table, on top of the Monet album. The catalog was open on a double-page spread with lingerie models. Roman recalled that his brother-in-law had brought this catalog to Maria as a gift from the US a couple of years ago.

Well, go figure! She has already explored the room, the little brat! thought Roman. He looked at the girl in confusion and, the longer he looked, the more anxious he felt. Her hair was scattered over the pillow, was she sick? He covered her legs with a woolen blanket and touched her head: her forehead was cold. He wanted to lie down next to her, to share his warmth with the girl. She must have missed the warmth of someone close.

It's too late to go anywhere. She can stay here overnight, Roman decided and went to the kitchen. Staring into the fuzzy darkness of the courtyard outside the window, he called Anna Pavlovna to let her know.

"Are you out of your mind?! You must return her tomorrow! You are putting us all at risk! Not a word about it to anyone else!" the Principal shouted angrily.

Roman stared at the full moon outside the window. He didn't feel like sleeping. He sighed and opened his laptop on the kitchen table and checked his e-mailbox. There was a message from his brother-in-law. His emails became infrequent after he had realized that it was useless to send such messages to Maria. Yet again, he urged them to leave the country before the borders were completely closed. He was convinced that the innocent era was over, and that Russia would soon come crashing down.

It is always easy to give advice. That was him who lost his nerve ten years ago. And what would I do abroad? All my relatives are here. I won't get drafted, that's for sure. I'll buy my way out of the service somehow. After all, the city needs me and, whatever they say, the market operates, Roman debated with himself. Eventually, in anger, he took a bottle of vodka out of the refrigerator.

Early in the morning, despite a severe headache, he took Vicky back to the orphanage. When they left the apartment and started down the stairs, Cleopatra Nikolaevna, an elderly talkative neighbor from the next floor down, watched them with suspicion.

On the way back, Vicky said that she had woken in the middle of the night to hear Roman washing dishes in the kitchen and occasionally sighing heavily. In the orphanage parking lot, she turned in the passenger seat, pecked Roman's unshaven cheek, and slipped out of the car. Astonished, Roman turned off the engine and watched for a long time as she skipped along the path covered with pine needles, until she disappeared around the corner.

Since then, the same thought was spinning in Roman's head: *I can't adopt her as a daughter. What can I offer her? Friendship? A friendship of a forty-two-year-old man with graying hair? Whoever would believe this? However, I care not about that; let them think what they want.*

After this incident, Vicky was silent for a whole week. Meanwhile, the eighteenth of August was approaching; it was the day when craftsmen celebrate an annual festival, the Ax Day. The festival took place in the Zertsalovo village, not far from the City-on-the-River. Roman promised to take the girl to the festival, to cheer her up a little. He told her stories about the ancestors who bore down and chopped their way through the taiga. With an ax, they could build a house and carve intricate window shutters. Quite unexpectedly, Roman received a short message from Anna Pavlovna just the day before the festival: the orphanage no longer needed his help. *What the hell is this all about?* he thought, unbelievingly, and he went anyway. But the guard firmly stopped him at the entrance:

"Excuse me! I am telling you clearly, listen to me! I have an order to not let you in! Don't be so pushy!"

Roman was so upset that he could do nothing right. Soon he was invited to discuss the construction project of the third municipal bridge, but he could barely follow what other experts were talking about in the City Council.

In early September, Roman was arrested on a grave charge of molestation of a minor. Maria, with a stony face, stared fixedly ahead and could not comprehend what was happening. She woke from a stupor, when her husband was being taken away in handcuffs, and pronounced her judgment in a strained voice:

"How could you, how could you? I told you that charity would not bring us anything good. It's all your **theory of small deeds**. You can't even live normally in your close circle, so how could you get involved with strangers?!"

During the apartment search, the police found a drawing of a girl in a short dress walking through a spring meadow and holding a yellow and blue ball above her head.

"We all fell victims of the hypnotic effect of his charm," Anna Pavlovna said when interviewed as a witness.

Roman sat in a jail cell on a cot leaning against a cold wall and thought: *This is a misunderstanding! I was falsely accused. What did I do wrong? What nonsense! After all, I'm an ordinary person; it may be said that I was re-born, I took a turn for a better life with all my heart, and experienced inspiration.*

At night, when he finally fell asleep, he dreamed that Vicky was once again in his apartment, but now it was him who was on the couch, and she covered him with some kind of sackcloth and said:

"If you can't adopt me, then you should marry me."

"But I'm married," Roman replied.

"I'll save you. Follow me; there should be a passage to the attic. Dragons are waiting on the roof. Let's fly away on them. We just need to cut a hole through the roof. Do you have an ax? You're a builder, a man."

Roman obeyed and followed the girl in fascination

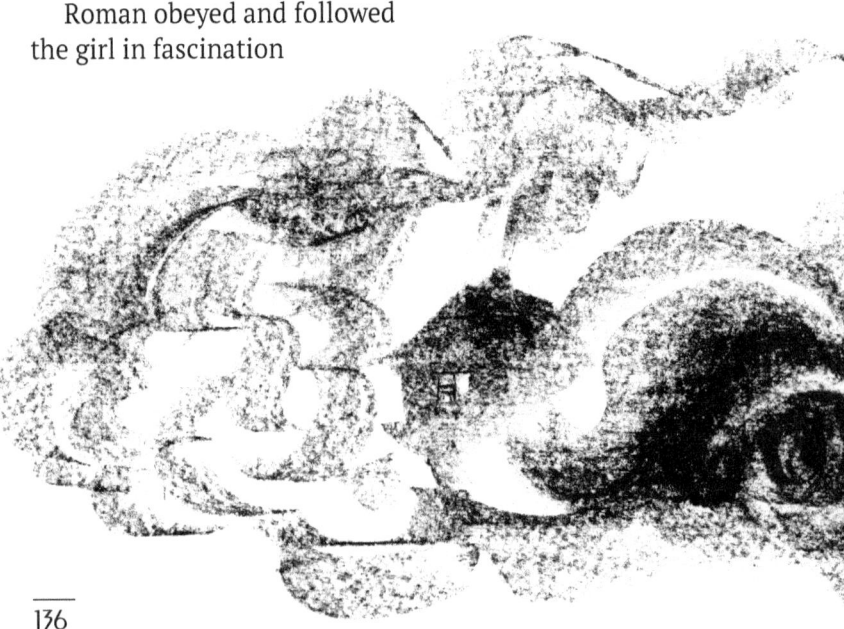

through a dark, damp tunnel, where the walls were covered with red-brown mold, and pearly mucus hung from the stone vaults. Then he groped for the ax inside his coat and wielded it. The wall silently collapsed in a cloud of scarlet dust. They were free.

When he woke up, he could not immediately distinguish between reality and nightmare. *Am I in love? But she's a child! What will I say during the interrogation? I am not Humbert Humbert[31]! It's laughable,* he thought.

The open gaze of the girl haunted him all morning. "Who was I to her?" he scolded himself.

Soon, Roman was summoned for an interrogation. He walked down the hallway on wobbly legs.

A man, clearly not from the prison staff — this was obvious from his clothes and behavior — picked up a sheet of paper covered in writing, and said:

"You must be aware that a verdict has already been prepared?" he narrowed his eyes and kept on searching for the appropriate lines:

"Well, hmm... The investigators indicated that you acted with premeditation in order to satisfy your sexual needs... Shall I continue?" He fixed his tenacious gaze on Roman and carefully placed the paper back on the table. "Anyway, consider yourself lucky. There has been an order. We need a foreman with knowledge of construction work to restore houses, bridges, roads, tram tracks, and other infrastructure."

For a moment the man was silent. Roman considered.

"Accept it! Otherwise you won't survive, what with your charges. You work, we reconsider the case, and hopefully there will be no trial. This case is quite complicated, Bastrykin[32] controls it himself," he coughed into his fist and added: "I hope I explained clearly enough?"

---

[31] Humbert Humbert is the protagonist of Vladimir Nabokov's novel *Lolita*.

[32] Alexander I. Bastrykin is the head of the Investigative Committee of Russia.

Roman imagined himself on the other side of the stone walls, in a shady park created by the unpaid prisoners' labor. There was even a small fountain in the park, where he went many times in his youth, and where a light breeze blew so pleasantly, and the smell of linden trees made his head spin. He remembered that, in his other life, he walked along the neatly paved path of this park and never even thought about the jail cells, with their smell of a grave.

"To build is not the same as to dig trenches. I'll do it," Roman answered in a shaky voice.

Immediately, he was overtaken with a feeling of tranquility, freedom, a beginning of a new life; his previous life faded away like a memory.

"Well, that's good! We are not monsters; we don't chop romantics' heads off. However, you would still have to eat some dust; there's nothing else to be done. You will have to work, so to speak, in our severe present," a satisfied smile flashed across the man's face.

Life at the Scarlet Sails orphanage was already on the fall schedule. In the mornings, the older children were driven to school; in the evenings, they gathered in the playroom. They were noisy.

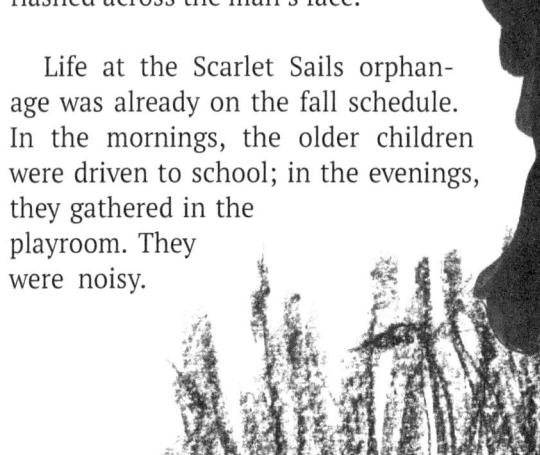

A teacher was fussing in the hall, explaining the rules of a new game to the children.

At eight o'clock in the evening, the orphanage guard ate cabbage soup with garlic, sitting at his small table covered with a checkered waterproof cloth. Glancing at the cuckoo clock, he straightened his back in an old man way, brushed back his sweaty hair, and walked through the corridor with his cheeks puffed out. From the door, leading to the large room, he spotted Vicky. He went up to her and said soothingly, stroking her hair:

"Don't worry, sweetheart, he will take you away as soon as he builds a house."

In the semi-darkness of the corridor, lanky Peter loitered.

THE LAST OLD WIVES' SUMMER

The end of September is Old Wives' Summer in Montana: gentle sunshine, blue sky, and transparent, warm air. A perfect time for relaxation!

"Alena from Golden Valley invited us to visit her. Perhaps, we can go?" my wife asked. "We've never been to their ranch before."

Knowing by word of mouth that Alena's husband was a horse breeder, I immediately agreed. My hidden motive was not the horses, or rather, not only them. For the past two years, we hadn't received many invitations, nor asked anyone to visit us.

Then the war began, followed by chronic depression. I didn't feel like doing anything. As soon as we woke up in the morning, we surfed the Internet immediately, looking for news about Ukraine. In March, people thought that the war would end by that summer; in the summer, that it would end by that fall; once the fall came, everyone had to realize that it would be a prolonged war, and we all needed to find a way to live with that fact. I took my attention away from heavy thoughts, spending my free time in the apiary with the bees, and my wife began to knit more. Hanging out with new Russian-speaking people was a brilliant idea! Let's go and have a good time.

It was almost twenty years ago that we moved to Bozeman, a small town between Yellowstone Park and the headwaters of the Missouri River. We both worked at the local university. Our children had grown and moved to big cities. But we enjoyed living here, in nature. The story in the movie *A River Runs Through It* starring Brad Pitt took place right around these parts. We lived in a one-story house with a mountain view. Sometimes we saw an air balloon floating in the distance. What a wide open space!

It was almost a three hour drive to Golden Valley; so we could be back that same night. After eating breakfast and taking our dog for a walk, we filled her food bowl for the day and hit the road. I brought a gift with me: a jar of fresh honey.

We took the freeway that crosses the States from west to east, and drove over the pass, beyond which there was a small town of Livingston on the banks of the Yellowstone River. Half a century ago, the famous Richard Brautigan lived at Pine Creek, not far from here; he was one of the last Beatniks, a participant in the Summer of Love events. Anyway, is it even worth envying those times when you are sixty years old?

We kept on going, enjoying the view. The Absaroka Range was to the right, and the Crazy Mountains were to the left in the distance, but there were miles and miles of endless withered prairie before them. In the latter half of the summer, rains were rare here. Pondering the mountains' names, I thought: *Isn't it crazy to go to a feast at a time of war?*

We had hardly covered a third of the way when we turned off the freeway close to the town of Big Timber, and leaving the mountains behind, drove north on the local highway to Harlowton. The gray prairie still stretched on both sides. We had taken this road a couple of times when we went fishing on the Missouri River. Today was the first time we turned east at Harlowton.

We called our friends: we are going to be late, no need to wait, start without us.

It was difficult to drive in anticipation of the feast. My wife knitted one of her "we'll see what it is when I'm done" projects, and somewhere along the way she offered to drive. I refused: what would I do if I didn't drive the car; I didn't know how to knit.

We saw more and more deer carcasses on the roadside. I started counting them: one, two, three... At some point, I gave this up deciding to focus on the road, so as to not hit a deer myself.

Finally, the GPS showed that we were not far from our destination. We turned onto a gravel road. I saw dilapidated trailers and abandoned rusty cars. A hope flashed through my mind that these were not our friends' abode. After winding around some mounds, the road led to a small hill. There sat a one-story sturdy log cabin; several cars were parked in the forest meadow. *This* matched the description.

The lady of the house welcomed us warmly and introduced us to the company. The guests were five Russian-speaking women from the area, all close to my age, give or take five years, who came without their American husbands. This was natural: after all, they wanted to have a light conversation in Russian without it being awkward.

The BBQ grill was lit behind the house. Jeff, the man of the house, was grilling burger patties. He was dressed in a light-colored shirt, blue jeans, and a leather belt with a large silver buckle. A short gray beard beautifully framed his chubby face. Jeff was a wounded Army veteran who decided to devote himself to his lifelong dream of breeding horses. "I dreamed of creating a new breed. Why not? I bought this large plot of land here." He made a grand gesture, and from this spot the property line was not even visible.

We went into the house. The huge table was already laid with cold and hot appetizers. Alena was the first to raise her glass. It turned out that this cabin was built specifically for parties with friends, and their family home stood further behind the hill. We had a toast to friends and chased it with red caviar on rye bread. Then there was a toast to peace. We drank and filled our plates with food. The women started sharing their culinary secrets.

After the hearty meal, Jeff suggested we take a walk and visit the horses. My wife and I, as well as two other female guests, joined the tour.

On the way, Jeff talked about his hobby. In his youth, he was not a diligent student. As a punishment, his strict father took away all books, except for textbooks. But Jeff escaped to the library, where he read anything and everything about horses. After graduating, he enlisted in the military. During the service, he tried to get to where the horses were.

We followed Jeff across a stretch of vacant land. Along the way, I plucked a twig of sagebrush and rubbed it in my palm: a fragrant smell of the prairie! By the roadside there was a frame of an old truck from the times of the Great Depression. The air was calm. I imagined that this frame, red with rust, would sing in a strong wind. It would sing with a voice of ages past! If I were a child, I would jump inside this colossal apparatus. I would turn the steering wheel, press the pedals, and look for the horn to honk: I wonder what kind of sound it would make.

We passed it by and entered the new century. It was a century of beautiful, pedigreed horses. I felt conflicted. It was the real Wild West! But it was so close to my heart! I closed my eyes for a second and breathed in deeply. It felt like I had landed in my home village.

Five minutes later, we saw the paddocks. It was clear that the horses felt free in this vast space. The abundantly manured

land was surrounded by steel strands of electric fences, sparkling in the sun, stretched along the perimeter from post to post for a good hundred yards.

Turning off the current with a master-switch and lifting the wire, Jeff ducked and stepped over to the animals' side. Standing there with his strong legs wide apart, he talked at length about the training methods and selection of horses, about their sale at horse shows. Sweat appeared on his forehead: he was older than me, somewhat overweight, and, moreover, his old wound appeared to be bothering him.

A beautiful young mare of dark color attracted my attention.

"What's her name?" I asked.

"Commander. My daughter named her," Jeff replied.

It would be Commandress *in Russian,* I thought.

There was a male horse in a separate enclosure. Noticing my interest, he approached and, wiggling his ears, straightened his neck. Scuffing the ground with his hooves, he snorted with his

wide nostrils and, shaking his head, suddenly turned his rear to me. Then he swept his tail to his wide flank, revealing the mighty groin of a stallion. Seeing this, Jeff punched the horse hard in the side: as a punishment, as he explained to me later.

When we returned to the table, it was getting dark. Svetlana, one of the guests, again made a toast to peace. I could not stand it anymore and, irritably adjusting my glasses, interjected:

"To peace? Okay, this is understandable, everyone wants peace. But let's be clear. What is peace? Perhaps, Russia should withdraw its troops from the territory of Ukraine? Then there will be peace!"

To my surprise, voices came from all around me:

"But what about Donbas? What about the Nazis? The Bandera supporters are there!"

My wife began to speak in my support, but the lady of the house, foreseeing the aggravation of the discussion, interrupted:

"We agreed not to talk about politics!"

I had to calm down. What could I do? We were at a party. After ten minutes my wife and I looked at each other and left the table, mentioning the lateness of the hour. It remained a mystery to me whether or not Jeff understood the gist of the conflict: the conversation was in Russian. But we shook hands warmly and arranged to go fishing next year.

The lady of the house and Rita from the town of Big Timber came out to accompany us to the car.

"We are with you on that one. But, you see, we have an agreement: not a word about politics. After all, we want some normal socializing, some warmth. See you later! We'll stay to chat with the girls for a bit longer." They smiled their goodbyes.

We were on our way. My wife said in disbelief, "How can they? Why, then, go into hiding in such a wilderness, on the other side of the Earth?"

I replied, "It is not surprising. It's globalization. Everything is intertwined, and other people will always be dark horses to us, so to speak."

The approaching darkness covered the prairie. There was no oncoming traffic, and I turned on the high beams.

We were silent the rest of the way.

That night I dreamed of a graceful white horse. The horse neighed.

The next morning, there was frost on the ground: the Second Summer was over.

I suddenly realized that, in fact, I had been living in emigration for a really long time.

The Prophetic Dreams of the Petrovs

O n a cloudy autumn morning of 1943, Ivan Petrov came down the steps of a sooty train car and walked through a small crowd in the station square. Out in the street, he adjusted his duffel bag on his back and walked awkwardly along a muddy sidewalk of the old city. His outward appearance did not surprise anyone: a military overcoat, worn-out kirza boots, and a garrison cap. His gaunt cheeks had not been shaven for a long time and were covered with overgrown stubble. *He must be on a short leave home,* a rare passer-by thought. However, looking into the face of this short man with his hair gone gray too early, one would feel uneasy: death looked out of his deep-set eyes.

Petrov turned from the main street into an alley lined with wooden buildings sitting on the edge of a gully. Fog flowed behind the buildings, settling to the gully bottom. It was eerily quiet, even lifeless, in this dead end, except for an occasional creak of a shutter, a lonely female voice from an open window, or a cat rustling along a blind fence and disappearing into a thicket of a huge burdock near a crooked gateway.

Petrov opened a footgate and walked into the courtyard of a two-story apartment building. Approaching the porch, he saw a lock on one of the entrance doors. He stood, confused, in the middle of the courtyard for a while, then wiped his face with his palm and, taking his burden off his shoulders, sat down on a worn bench under the window. He took out a pouch of tobacco from the cuff of his overcoat, slowly rolled a cigarette, and lit it.

My ninety-year-old mother recalled, "I came home from school. I saw a stranger sitting outside the apartment; he asked if he could spend the night. I didn't know whether to let him in or not." I'd gone to visit my mother just before Victory Day that year. "And he was... nothing but skin and bones; death is usually pictured like this. I looked at him and I felt sorry for him. I decided to let him stay, but to keep an eye on him all night: he was a total stranger. I was eleven years old." Mom shrugged her lean shoulders and continued after a pause: "I stared at him for a long time. His eyes were not unlike my dad's. After a moment he couldn't contain himself anymore and said:

"Oh, daughter, how quickly you forgot me."

Petrov and his daughter went inside. A neighbor peeked in and exclaimed:

"Goodness gracious! Ivan? You are alive! You look just like Hitler!"

"They didn't feed me that much," he joked, coughing into his fist.

Soon Marfa, Ivan's wife, returned. She clasped her hands, hugged him, and began to cry. Then she wiped away her tears and laughed.

"I was feeling lonely. The other night, I had *a dream*. At first I thought it was a bad dream," she admitted. "As if a gypsy — I couldn't make out her face — foretold: **your husband will come back from the war, but you won't be there to welcome him.**"

"Had I known, I would have waited around the corner," Ivan quipped again.

To a stranger it may have seemed that Petrov was constantly winking, but it wasn't the case. He had a ptosis of his right eye from birth.

After some time, the eldest daughter Galya came home from school.

"You will hardly gain any weight on what food we have. Galya lost our food vouchers recently. Thank God, it's the end of the month. I think you should go to my step-sister, Anna, it will be better for you in the countryside, and they will have more food," said Marfa. "And I'll join you with the girls after I get the new food vouchers and do some shopping."

Galya felt guilty and was upset that her father had to leave again.

Two days later the Petrovs went to the open-air market. They spent a long time looking for a produce wagon that was returning to the collective farm named "Beacon of Communism", or simply "Beacon". Eventually, they found one near the old warehouses and persuaded the driver to give Ivan a ride: such an emaciated man could hardly walk twenty-five miles, they said.

The wagon driver, an elderly woman with a pockmarked face and a shadow of a mustache above her upper lip, generously agreed. Ivan threw his pack onto the cart and then, awkwardly, threw his bones in next to his belongings. Tucking up the hem of her long gypsy skirt, the driver sat on the front edge, clicked her tongue loudly, and shook the reins. Snorting, the horse obediently moved off.

They left the city by the Irkutsk Tract. It was drizzling. The driver was silent for a long time, gloomily looking ahead, half-heartedly urging on her sluggish dobbin. Ivan sat to the side and slightly behind the woman, dozing and muttering something: the steady ride lulled him to sleep. Only when they reached the village of Surovo, the silence was broken.

"We have run out of flour at home, and the collective farm doesn't give us more. They say we haven't fulfilled the production plans, although we have been working day and night.

I need to feed the children somehow. I had to sell a few things to buy some flour," she nodded at the small bag. "Almost all collective farm horses were taken to the war. I begged them to give me this old nag. What's your story? Wounded?" the driver asked, glancing at Ivan.

"The wound is nothing, just a scratch. We were surrounded. At first we were glad that we had survived, but when we began to starve, we envied those who had been killed by bullets. We were too weak to dig graves. We slept next to the corpses. I don't even want to remember," he turned his head away; the moisture from the rain glistened on his cheeks.

Splashing through puddles and bouncing heavily in the ruts, the cart turned off the main road. They drove for another five miles. Finally, they stopped at a junction.

"Well, Godspeed," Ivan said goodbye and, shouldering his pack, set off down the familiar road.

It was getting dark. A bonfire was burning in the distance. The road ran between harvested fields and copses of trees turning yellow. Ivan mentally revisited these lands, where he grew up scything grass with his brothers and sisters, and watching cattle graze at night with his buddies. Then he got married and had children. In order to give them an education, they moved to the city. They made it out just in time, before collectivization. Looking back, Ivan figured that he first met Anna about ten years ago; he couldn't tell exactly. It was at haying time. He had already married Marfa, and Anna was still very young, although she looked much older than her fifteen years. She was walking across the meadow in the first row of women, turning the cut grass with a rake.

Finally, the village appeared around the bend. Anna's house stood on the edge, near a copse of birches, with two windows looking out onto a harvested field. Pushing the unlocked door with his shoulder, Ivan let himself in. Clearing his throat loudly at the threshold, he briefly glanced around the room, dimly lit by a light bulb without a lampshade: the floor — unpainted and scrubbed until it was yellow, a bench, and a small, sturdy table by the window.

In response to the noise, a young woman hurried out from the next room, separated from the kitchen by a Russian stove. She did not immediately recognize the newcomer standing in the semi-darkness of the hallway: only the familiar squint of his right eye gave him away. At first, Anna shied away in disbelief: he had changed so much.

"Well, since you already came in, welcome!" she invited, quickly hugging him with her tanned, sinewy arms.

A fair-haired boy of about six ran out from behind the stove and, stamping his foot, stood at a distance.

"Here is my Lyonya. Come here, don't be afraid, this is Uncle Vanya," Anna called her son to her and stroked his hair.

The next morning, leaving for work, she instructed Ivan to heat the bath-house and fetch water from the stream that flowed behind the vegetable garden.

That day Anna returned home earlier than usual. She gave Ivan some of her husband's clean clothes, which she had neatly kept in a chest all the years since his death.

In the front room of the bath-house, Ivan stripped naked. He examined himself: his arms and legs were whole; the only scar was on his left shoulder, where he was hit by shrapnel. *I can still live and fight,* he thought.

The door burst open. Anna came in wearing only her nightgown.

"Well, my hero, lie down on the bench with your tail under the bench. I'll put you back on your feet in a blink, and you'll be a real man," she said, slightly pushing Ivan forward, and closed the door tightly behind her.

"As you say... I'm a man, though, am I not?" Ivan chuckled and obediently stretched out his naked body on the wooden shelf, belly down.

Anna scooped up boiling water with a ladle and splashed it on the heater. Thick steam filled the space of the bath-house and swirled under the low ceiling. Then she took a soaked birch sauna whisk out of the basin, shook it over Ivan's body and began to whip his back, buttocks, thin thighs, and calloused heels.

"Have mercy on the old soldier," he soon begged, breathing heavily.

"Now flip to your back," she said in a friendly tone and threw some more water on the hot stones.

Ivan turned over with difficulty and covered his groin with his hands. Through the steam, he saw young breasts under a wet shirt hovering over him and, closing his eyes, he entrusted himself to this woman. She continued to whisk him diligently with twigs over his entire body: from his ankles to his shoulders, while carefully avoiding the wound on his arm.

"That's enough for the first time," Anna said and having doused Ivan with cold water from a bucket, opened the door wide.

Ivan caught his breath and slowly moved to the anteroom. There was a strong pounding in his temples. He hadn't been to a bath-house for over a year! He blew his nose with pleasure into a rag. He returned to the house in long johns and a long, almost knee-length, canvas shirt. Anna handed him a mug of kvass.

He drank it in one gulp, wiped his still unshaven face with his sleeve and asked playfully, leaning on the doorframe:

"The kvass is so good. How do you make it?"

"After you live with me one, two, and then three days, I'll teach you."

"I'm really drowsy all of a sudden. Make me a bed behind the stove," said Ivan.

It's like being born again. Just recently I was tearing my flesh with my nails, he thought, lying down on the cot, and soon fell asleep.

New disasters appeared in his dreams: **Huge machines without people flew into the sky like birds, and people fled from their exhaust flames. The survivors ran out of their homes, scattering around grain. Blood flowed everywhere, while he himself was steering a horse. Huge fissures appeared here and there in the ground. People shouted something to him, but he did not understand their foreign language and, whipping the horse, kept on riding to his death.**

Ivan uttered a scream and woke up.

"Vanya, what's wrong? "Anna asked quietly, coming up to his bed.

"I saw in a dream that I was plowing the ground, but, it seems, I fell under a plow," Ivan answered, rising on his elbow from the sheepskin. And then suddenly, as if having absorbed the power of animal fur, he possessively pulled Anna towards him. The next moment, his right hand penetrated her wet groin. She grabbed his waist, breathing heavily, and smell-

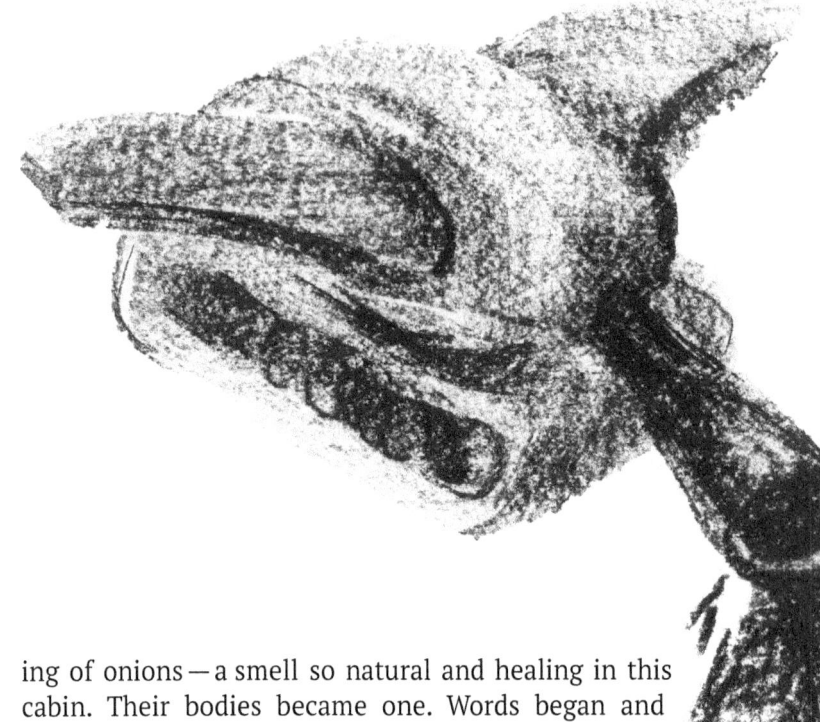

ing of onions — a smell so natural and healing in this cabin. Their bodies became one. Words began and ended, turning into short moans, until both fell silent and still. Briefly, Ivan woke up from his dozing and felt Anna quietly stroking the scar on his shoulder with her finger.

Was this really a dream? he thought and mentally made the sign of the cross. Then he fell asleep again, without any dreams this time. His loud snoring filled the house.

Soon the entire village knew that Ivan, back from the war, emaciated, was stay-ing with Anna. Everyone brought what they could: a chicken egg here, a small chunk of bacon there,

156

half of a roasted hare, a jug of milk with a pie, and someone treated him to potato pancakes.

At first, Ivan got up from the cot only to eat and go to the outhouse. He ate with concentration, without haste. Every day, he was looking more alive. Regaining his strength, he began to leave the house. Once he took a hammer and nails and repaired the rickety fence. A week later, he began to notice little Lyonya, who was shy of the guest at first; the boy looked at him from the top of the woodstove or hid in the far corner of the room, where he sat hugging his knees with his hands. The boy soon became bolder and once asked Ivan: "Will you be my dad?"

Anna always returned from work at the collective farm in the evening. Ivan, clean-shaven and fresh, waited for her at the door and told her how he and Lyonya had cut willow branches and, weaving a basket to catch fish out of them, threw the basket into a backwater of the river not far from the village. The next day they would go and check how big the catch was.

Anna listened and smiled, exhausted.

"The production demands are so high," she complained. "Sometimes you milk a lot of milk, pour it into cans, and they take it all to the city for processing. There's almost nothing left for us. Over the summer, I was completely beat from work in hot weather. I collected rye into sheaves following the harvester, and then I, stooped, labored in the potato fields. It was rough. It took everything I had. I would return from the fields in the dark and have no time left to go gather mushrooms and wild berries. Thank God, the farm gave me some flour and delivered firewood for the winter."

"You have never visited since you left for your city," she grinned after a pause. "My Mikhail was loud and rowdy, and he wasn't gentle, but he was hard-working. When the war with the Finns began, he walked around gloomily, as if he knew that he would be drafted and would not return. Maybe he froze to death, who knows..."

They were silent. Anna did not mention her late husband again, and this made Ivan feel comfortable. He asked:

"What have you heard about Kolka?"

"He is missing in action. Well, it serves him right! One winter he got drunk and kicked his wife and baby out into the street. They hid in a hog house, and afterwards got sick and then died."

"What about Stasik?"

"They sent him to the front, to the Polish Army. He is our enemy now. In 1941, he was worried that if the Germans did not have enough strength to reach the Urals, he would never return home."

"Him, an enemy?! I remember him wearing bast shoes and a rope for a belt."

"Clearly, he was not a kulak. Needless to say, there are almost no men left in the village; only the lame Gotka and the crazy Ilya."

It was Second Summer. The wind from the open window gently ruffled the curtain: a reminder that warm days would soon end. Fixing his gaze on a strip of light that expanded onto a field, Ivan watched the last ray disappear. He did not want to remember the past or think about the war anymore.

A few days later it began snowing. Large flakes fell and immediately melted on the weeping ground. There was no sign of Marfa and his daughters.

Meanwhile, the war went on. There were the battles of Donbass and for the liberation of Crimea.

Ivan sometimes thought that he would be sent back to the front and never see the village again.

"A few months after Father was called back to the war, his letter came from Riga," my mom continued the story. "He wrote that being a rifleman was not at all like serving in a construction battalion. He was wounded, but not seriously, and he was well fed and cared for in the hospital. He also wrote that he would soon go and finish off the Nazis. There was a photo enclosed: he looked healthy, and it was clear that he had not been going hungry. He came back from the war wearing officer's boots and a new uniform blouse; he brought us gifts, things he had taken as war trophies, and among them was a beautiful dress for my mother. He said that he had carried a German-made carpet, but was forced to sell it on the way back home to buy food. The trip was so long, across the whole country. Later, he returned to the village and became a hunter; he usually bagged foxes and squirrels. Anna bore him three children. My mother, my sister Galya and I lived in the town. Mother sometimes cried: she felt slighted. But we, the daughters, did not hold it against Father."

I carefully wrote down my mother's stories, remembering the village where I visited every summer as a child and where I was bored to tears and missed home badly. I remembered the flies in grandma Anna's house that drove me crazy so I frantically squished them with a newspaper on the window. Sometimes, at night, I secretly tried to smoke behind the garden. Grandpa Ivan did not talk about the war and, to my questions, only said: "Ah, Grandson, Grandson..." Occasionally, we went mushroom picking together. Grandpa cut each mushroom, carefully examined the cut, and if he found a wormhole, he carefully cleaned it with a sharp knife, saying: "And I will send these mushrooms to Marfa in town. She likes them clean and sturdy."

"What happened to Lyonya?" I asked my mother, remembering that by that time Lyonya no longer lived in the village.

"He got an engineering degree. He worked at the secret city called "Pyaty Pochtovy". There was an accident with the nuclear reactor, and he died from radiation sickness soon after. Well, I'm tired now. Go check the mailbox, son," my mother requested.

Putting aside my notebook and pen, I went out onto the landing and walked down two floors. In the mailbox I found a utility bill and an envelope without any address.

"A Victory Day card, maybe?" my mom pointed to the anonymous message.

I opened the envelope. It contained a letter from a Hero of Russia with an appeal to enlist in the Wagner PMC[33] and fight in the Special Military Operation in Ukraine.

"Obviously, a mistake," Mother suggested. "I'm ninety; I've lived long on the face of this earth. Let others fight."

Then, after a minute of contemplation, she whispered urgently:

"Don't you even think about joining them!"

"What are you talking about, Mom! It's high time we ended this merry-go-round. We've fought enough. Time to live in peace now," I said with a hint of bitter pacifism that we have not yet fully explored.

---

[33] A private military company.

A Walk with a Sketch Map

A flower blooms when I see you.
The breeze rustles in the poplar tree when I hear you.
I fall into the abyss when I think about you.
It's easy to fly into the abyss:
What space, what freedom there is in infinity!
I fly and break into fragments.
I take a detached view — I seem to be a whole person, but
  as soon as one gets closer, so close that one can't even
  see the clothes, absolutely nothing is whole.
Everything is exploding and scattering, as if it were just
  after the Big Bang.
How can I get reassembled? Where can I find the center of
  gravity, where will the fragments of my inner galaxy fly?
Or maybe I've already succumbed to the force of gravity
  and every element in my veins makes me live...
When I get close, I move away.
When I move away, I get closer.

If you ever had to travel in a half-empty suburban bus, then you can easily imagine the following scene.

It is winter. A young man in a thick black woolen coat rides an unheated bus Route 18 to the Institute of Morphogenesis at the Sputnik stop. He takes a spot by a window, on a seat covered in worn-out fake leather. He holds a wide one-quart jar in his lap. The glass container is filled with a liquid with human embryonic tissue and tightly closed with a polyethylene lid. The bus sways on the rough road, and the white fibers of the tissue swirl, forming a helical structure.

In another seat, a hunched, bespectacled man is absorbed in a three-dimensional matrix of a text: *Fractal analysis can be used to assess the self-similar dimension of morpho-functional blocks. If the block sizes are multiples of the Fibonacci sequence of digits 1, 1, 2, 3, 5, then...* Mulling over the meaning of what he has just read and trying to connect it with the world around him, he clenches his fist and presses it against the frosted window. A crescent-shaped patch appears on the glass. He adds five thumb prints to the patch, and it turns into an approximation of a child's footprint.

I am one of those men.

The bus keeps rolling along a forest. Parallel to the road, under bright lights, there is a cross-country ski track, and the silhouettes of skiing enthusiasts glide along it. I would not mind skiing this magical track.

The bus conductor, a woman in a fluffy woolen shawl, watches thoughtfully as the tops of the pine trees flicker in and out beyond the window. A leather bag with a roll of tickets hangs on her chest, and there are wings behind her back. The crisscross lights create such bizarre shadows.

I am getting drowsy. I listen to the monotonous sound of the wheels, and through

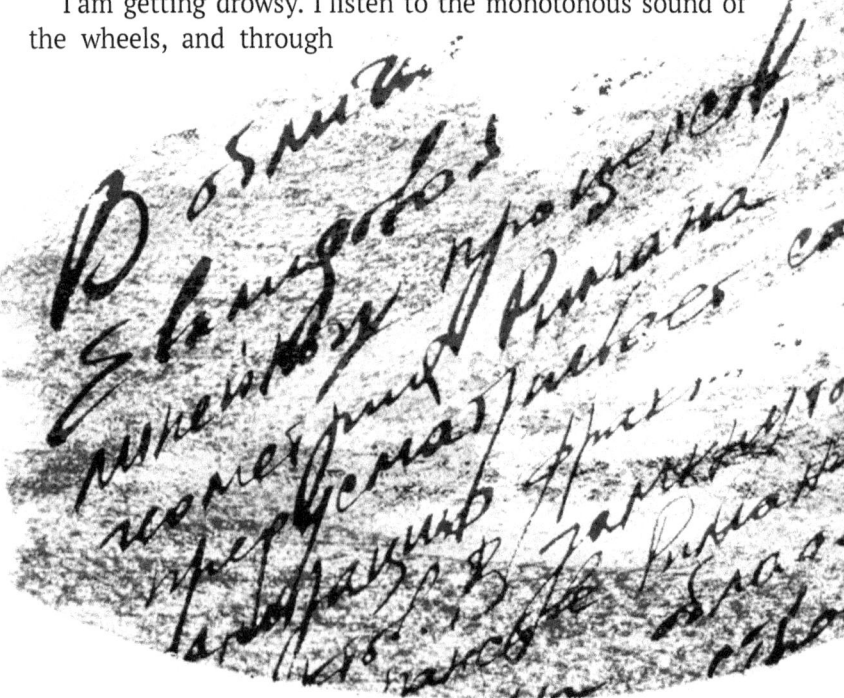

half-
closed
eyes I see a
cube-shaped head on
the driver's shoulders.
Light comes from this cube,
like a spotlight, illuminating tree
trunks on the way. They cast a con-
tinuous barcode onto the turquoise snow.
This creates the illusion of movement. In fact,
all the changes in this century have already ended. Only other states of matter remain.
My eyes close. I dream of hiking in the taiga once,
in summer.

Around eleven o'clock at night after a difficult hike through a peat bog overgrown with dwarf Arctic birch, I decided to take a break and consult the sketch map of the area. At this point, the expedition trail followed the curve of a foothill; a ridge rose above the horizon. A carpet of Reindeer moss glowed silver in the cold rays of the full moon. I approached a boulder field and wearily put my foot on the ledge of a large rock to tighten the laces of my messy foot wraps, called *onuchi*. Other stones were much smaller, about one to two inches in diameter. Before I bent down, I caught sight of a flash high in the sky. A meteor flew through the dark expanse of the night. *Now it will burn out and disappear,* I thought. But the closer it approached, the brighter it burned and the slower it fell. I was so fascinated, I did not have time to make a wish, like I had be-

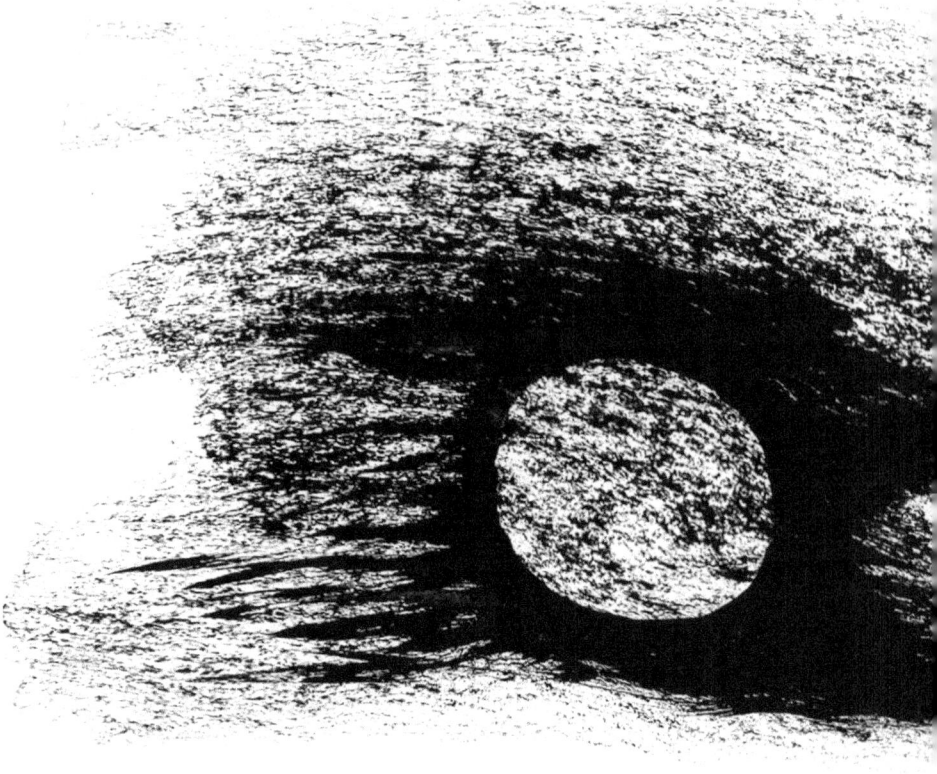

fore, in my youth. A second later, it silently landed on a scattering of stones, as if it were not a meteorite but the first stage of a rocket booster.

Picking up the melted hot body the size of a quail egg, I took a minute to explore the purple streaks on the slightly bumpy surface. It radiated an enormous heat, but my palm did not feel any pain. After a moment, I put it down on the ground. There was no sign of a burn on my hand. I closed my eyes, and when I opened them again, I realized that I could no longer distinguish the alien rock from the rest of similarly dark gray stones.

My capacity for analytical thinking was finally restored, and I began to worry: *They could disqualify me and forbid me to work in this region.* I hadn't taken any samples. It was clear that I was not ready for my mission.

After adjusting the straps of my backpack, I headed west. The huge moon was visible over the swamp. I saw mossy, sagging fir trees, and stars lit up in the sky one after another.

As I walked, enjoying the beauty of the landscape, I realized that I had not seen the blazes on trees for a long time,

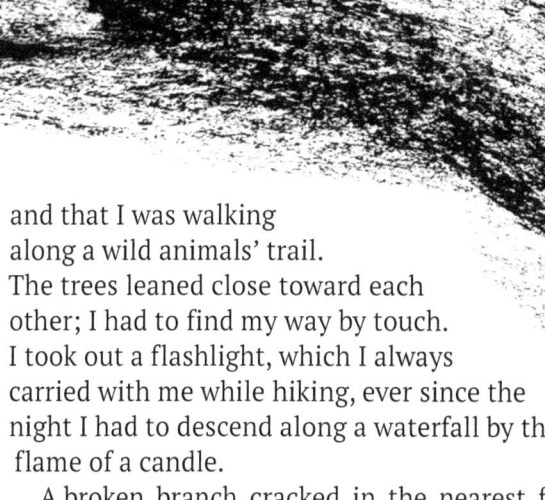

and that I was walking
along a wild animals' trail.
The trees leaned close toward each
other; I had to find my way by touch.
I took out a flashlight, which I always
carried with me while hiking, ever since the
night I had to descend along a waterfall by the
 flame of a candle.

A broken branch cracked in the nearest fir grove.
The beam of the flashlight caught the eyes of a deer
standing among the trees.

Holding my breath, I returned to the path, which in a hundred yards led me to a small lake. Apparently, animals watered there. The forest opened up, and although the moon shone brightly, I decided it would be more prudent to start searching for my trail in the morning.

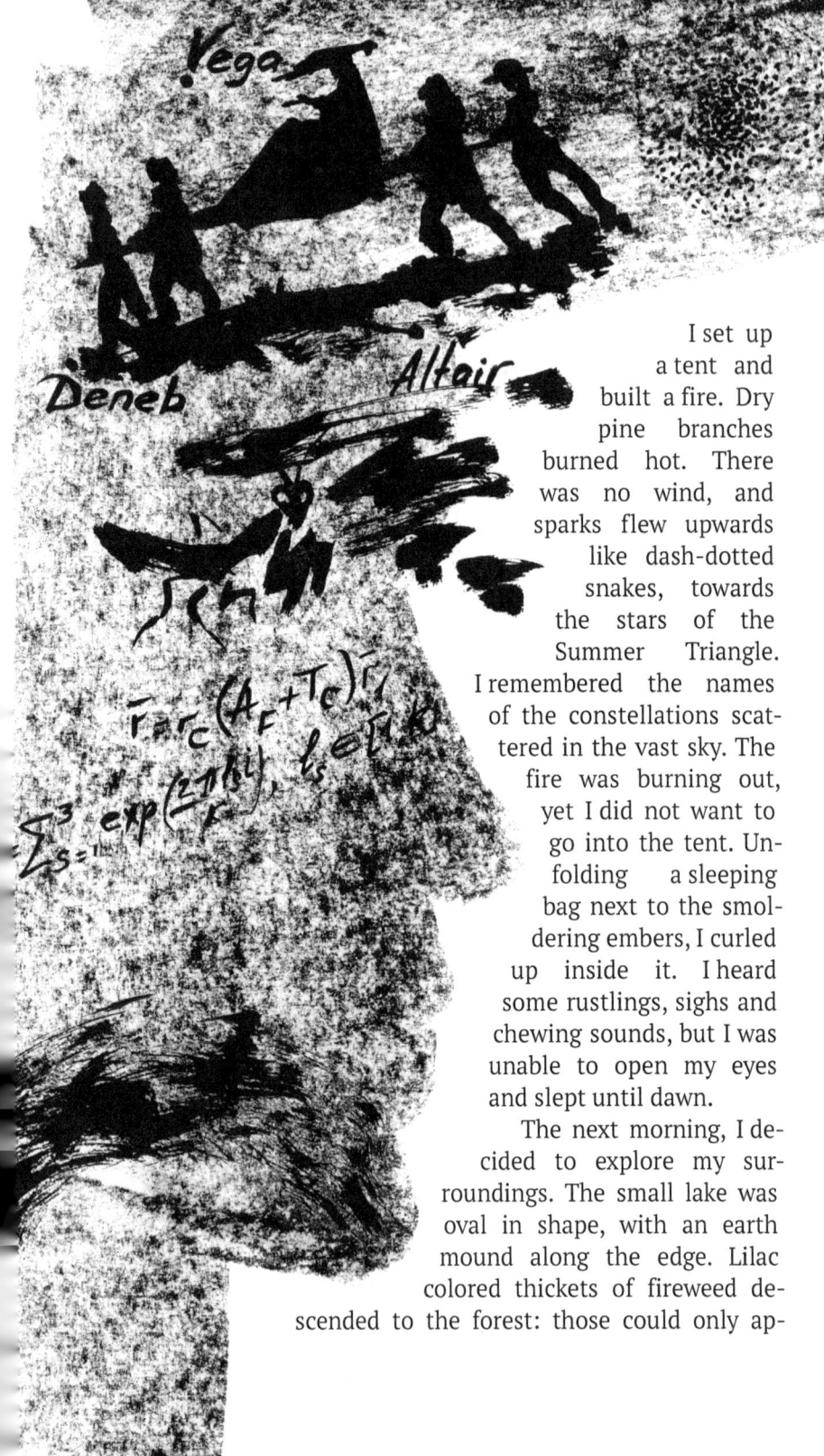

Vega

Deneb   Altair

$$\bar{\tau} = \tau_C (A_F + T_C)\tau_1$$

$$\sum_{s=1}^{3} \exp\left(\frac{27\pi}{x}\right), \, l_s \cdot \cdots$$

I set up a tent and built a fire. Dry pine branches burned hot. There was no wind, and sparks flew upwards like dash-dotted snakes, towards the stars of the Summer Triangle. I remembered the names of the constellations scattered in the vast sky. The fire was burning out, yet I did not want to go into the tent. Unfolding a sleeping bag next to the smoldering embers, I curled up inside it. I heard some rustlings, sighs and chewing sounds, but I was unable to open my eyes and slept until dawn.

The next morning, I decided to explore my surroundings. The small lake was oval in shape, with an earth mound along the edge. Lilac colored thickets of fireweed descended to the forest: those could only appear after a fire. Indeed, the bark on the trees was burned, and some larch trees had fallen away from the lake. I imagined the crashing sound of falling trunks. Despite the swarms of bloodsuckers, I quickly undressed and entered the water. A black swan with an elegantly curved neck swam out from behind a snag, accelerated with a few beats of its wings and flew up over the shrub wood with a trumpet call. My heart kept beating steadily, as if it was a common occurrence.

With small steps, I went further, pushing water with my hands. It had already risen to my chin. I felt with my feet when the bottom dropped off. The abundance of humic acids in the water made it resemble strong black tea. I had to admit that it would not be possible to solve the question about karstic or other origin of the water basin without having special equipment, or a sampling of soil or bottom ooze.

Out of the water and dressed, I easily climbed a tall old pine tree. The pristine taiga stretched for dozens of miles in all directions. A mountain rose in the west. There should be a river down in the valley before it.

A squirrel brushed by me on a nearby branch, lightly touching the back of my head with its ginger tail. I was so startled that I almost lost my balance. The squirrel squeaked somewhere in the treetop, expressing its irritation at the intruder. Wishing her well, I carefully climbed down, and as soon as I touched the ground, I discovered an old blaze on a nearby tree: an Evenki path ran along a dry hillock ahead. I packed my things into my backpack and almost ran along the path, leaving behind only the cold ash of the campfire.

A few hours later, I reached the river, whose beauty was the subject of many hymns. A crossing over the riffles was nearby. Four strong men in wet weatherproof jackets walked towards the bank and carried a palanquin made of spindly trunks of young pines. On the palanquin sat Hannah. Her fingers clutched an elaborate cigarette holder, and when she brought her hand to her lips, the sleeve of her windbreaker dropped away, revealing her tattooed forearm: a Mandelbrot Fractal, well-known to me.

I took the place of one of the carriers. The palanquin was wider than the path, and our feet struggled through the bushes. From time to time one of us sank knee-deep into the bog, and the others had to squat to keep the makeshift palanquin horizontal. It was drizzling. We walked the mile to the base in three hours, now and then stopping for interchanges and breathers.

We called for the helicopter on a portable radio. By evening, it hovered over the swamp, dispersing the clouds of heavy rain. Hiding her excitement, Hannah smiled: the flight would pass over the abyss of the Great Basin. Holding her purple hat by the brim, she vanished into the hatch of the steel bird. I passed the bag with samples to the co-pilot and retreated. The helicopter took off. Branches of wild rosemary with white flowers swayed wildly in the wind. I was tipped over, as if I were a cardboard cut-out of a man. I fell into the embrace of the sphagnum moss. The clouds kept on floating as if in a silent movie.

I stayed on the ground for a long time until I spotted a common praying mantis. It turned its triangular head in a funny way, tilting it to one side or the other as if to make sure I was watching it. I rolled over and suddenly began saying again and again, "Mantis, I love you; and you, oh green mountain, are beautiful!"

Nature went still at my mumbling. The mist cleared away, and the pine tree tops glowed in the golden rays of the setting sun.

I opened my eyes when the conductor announced, "Sputnik stop. End of the line!"

Cheryomushki Club

I t was late September. Cold drizzle had persisted all week, and the night before there was a hard freeze. The roads shone with silver ice. There could be up to forty car accidents in our Siberian city on days like that, some tragic. Drivers called that period the Tinsmith's Days, half in jest, but Alina believed since recently that this particular example of jargon was inappropriate.

Car owners rushed to change into snow tires...

Early in the morning, Alina drove her old Lada to the auto-shop. The sign on the fence briefly announced: "Tire Service". For the first time in a long time, the girl smiled, remembering that as a child she used to love reading signs backwards.

The work was expected to take a half hour, and Alina decided to go for a walk and explore. It was her first time in this part of the city, almost the suburbs. The sidewalk had seen better days. The puddles in the potholes were covered with ice with heaps of rusty leaves frozen in it.

Alina walked, breaking the thin ice with the heels of her boots, and thought: *If Yurik had had snow tires on a year ago, maybe the accident wouldn't have happened.*

That morning, they drove from their home village to the city. Yurik was at the wheel. Fog was thinning outside the window, and nothing told them that those were their last moments together.

"Oh no, what's that?!" Alina only had time to shout out in fear when, on a slight curve, their car suddenly skidded and crashed into the bumper of an oncoming truck at full speed. The impact was so hard that Yurik was ejected through the windshield.

Everything was still for a second. The two vehicles were smoking on the side of the road. A frosty, alien forest rose tall behind them, and snowflakes fell slowly.

The firefighters, the EMERCOM team, and the ambulance arrived. The emergency response group got the unconscious girl out of the crumpled car. Her legs were broken. She, unlike the driver, had had her seatbelt on, and lived.

Alina woke up in a local hospital. She had lost a lot of blood and only miraculously survived: matching donor blood had been found quickly. Immobilized, she underwent osteosynthesis surgery: titanium plates were installed on her tibias.

Her career in sports was over. Before, she and Yurik were the best on their local biathlon team! She sank deep into depression.

Alina did not see any point in staying in her village. She moved to the city six months after the terrible accident to study agriculture at the university. Her mother saw Alina off

with tears and clumsily suppressed joy; her heart was filled with pride and hope that Alina would get a higher education and make something of herself.

Alina's father had been gone for two years by then. The manner of his death was common for a Russian rural area: he went fishing, drank vodka, fell overboard, got tangled in the fishing gear, and drowned.

Alina loved her father and had a very close bond with him. He taught her how to ski, swim, drive, and shoot a hunting rifle. He told her that, as a young man, he watched the Chulym meteorite[34] pass in the sky, with a fiery tail, and saw the fire-ball of the explosion in the air; later, that spring, he went to the taiga in search of its fragments. He enjoyed making things with his hands and sometimes built birdhouses. How they rejoiced together at birds moving in in the spring! For a time, her father taught a woodworking class at the high school, but then he quit and set up a carpentry workshop in the village; the shop brought considerable, by local standards, income to their family. Everything was good, until her mother found out that he had cheated on her. The domestic quarrels got gradually worse, and her father began to drink more and more often, and he would leave to go hunting or fishing alone on weekends.

Deep in thought, Alina walked along an oxbow lake, nick-named Chokecherry Backwater, and at the tram terminus she stepped onto a wooden bridge and from there deftly jumped down onto a sandy path that led to a low hill. There was a wonderful view of the wide river valley with gantry cranes unloading barges. Only a few days were left before navigation ended.

Alina looked down, where the fastest waters of the stream sparkled freely and cheerfully in the sun's rays, and realized that her village lay a hundred miles to the north, downstream from that bend; perhaps, those barges with timber arrived from there.

What peace! she thought in admiration and, after standing for a minute near a large smooth boulder, quickly walked back. A westerly breeze blew, carrying with it the rotten smell of the swamp from the backwater. On the opposite bank of that enclosed, crescent-shaped pond, the dome of the bell tower sparkled. Wooden houses in the single-family residential neighborhood were scattered down the gentle slope from the church.

---

[34] The cosmic body entered the Earth's atmosphere on the evening of February 26, 1984 and burned up at an altitude of about 60 miles in the area of the Chulym River (a tributary of the Ob River) on the border of the Krasnoyarsk Territory and the Tomsk Region.

When Alina got back to the tire shop, her Lada with snow tires on was already out in the parking lot. She paid and, getting behind the wheel, noticed a newly built three-story mansion of red brick with pilasters at a distance. A young man in an elegant cashmere coat pressed the bell button at the entrance. The iron door opened immediately, as if he had been expected, and he disappeared inside.

Alina was curious. In her parked car, she entered the following address into her iPhone: 232 Mir Avenue. The browser returned: "Tire Service", and below, at the same address: "Cheryomushki[35] Club, men only, 24/7: hookah, striptease, erotic massage."

Here's the **Ecivres Erit,** Alina smirked, looking in the rearview mirror, and started the car. Turning onto the avenue, she checked the brakes on the icy road: everything worked as it should.

Alina was a freshman at the university. The scholarship was meager, and she got a job as a florist in a flower shop, where she created bouquets and fancy ikebanas. At first the work seemed interesting. One day, a strange customer in dark glasses came in and ordered a bouquet with a meaning: "An elderly tiger puts his paw on the chest of a young doe." Alina had enough imagination to make a composition from delicate and, in her opinion, from more austere and proud flowers. Another Romeo bought twenty-five red roses and asked her to partially cut the stems just under the blooms. He wanted to impress his girlfriend: at the moment she unwrapped the bouquet, all the buds but one would fall. Alina refused; she did not have the heart to mutilate the flowers.

This is so shallow! Go to hell! she mentally kicked the buyer out.

After paying rent, there was little left of her salary. Once a month she went to visit her mother. She didn't date, but at night she felt an unexpressed hunger for intimate touch.

---

[35] The name of objects, most often regions and settlements, associated with the chokecherry plant in the former USSR.

A week later she called the Cheryomushki Club and arranged for a job interview.

The first fluffy snow fell that day. Alina approached the familiar mansion on the northern outskirts of the city. A black foreign-made car, lightly dusted with silver, stood by the fence.

Straining to pull the iron door open, she entered a dim corridor, where doors to rooms were arranged in a checkerboard pattern. At the very end there was a mirror. Cold purple light poured from hidden sources, promising sensual pleasure to new clients.

Cool walls, Alina noted.

She was invited into the room closest to the exit. There were unoccupied soft leather sofas around the perimeter, and a ghostly pole glittered in the center.

Showing herself off was not difficult. Alina was a slim blonde with a wide face, slanted green eyes and an upturned nose; she made a graceful curtsey, demonstrated flexibility at the pole, and answered questions calmly and confidently. She was unanimously accepted as a qualified *master*, and hired. She was instructed in the basic techniques for bringing a client to orgasm.

Later, Alina met the other girls of the Club. All were between eighteen and twenty-five years old. Each had her own club nickname: big-eyed Eva; languid Mila; slender Isabelle; fast as a whirlwind, Catherine; seductive Vasilisa; pale-skinned

Snezhana, beautiful in her touching nudity. The administrator was nicknamed the Queen by the girls. "Don't get into arguments with clients! Convince them with your hands! And they can't escape your hands!" She mentored the girls.

There was a kitchen in one of the mansion rooms. Here they could have a snack and check their iPhone. One could see the bell tower from the window overlooking the backyard.

"This is the Temple of St. Sergius of Radonezh. A fragment of his remains is kept there," the Queen once explained. She practiced

meditation and yoga and loved to talk about the third eye, aura, chakras, subtle body, energy flows, and vibrations. "However, it is not the subtle body and vibrations that our clients need, but attention and feminine affection..." she slyly added in a chesty, raspy voice, hurrying out into the corridor after the next client called.

The Queen had the price list memorized. Everything had its price: the hookah, striptease, contrast whirlpool tub for water seekers,[36] erotic massage without touching the girl, Tantric and Thai massages; and the same with two *masters*. The available services were full of surprises: "golden shower", "lotus stamens", "pearl necklace", and so on. Every type, place, and method of contact had its own tariff. Most men couldn't help but respond in kind. And then the cash register was filled.

The sweet languor of the morning gradually gave way to a flood of visitors in the evening. Some of them were self-confident, arrogant, with shaved heads; the others were awkward and shy, with a timid smile and downcast gaze. It was clear that they had never harassed women, never touched or groped them. These men had to be taught that, in fact, they could run their hands all over within certain limits, in order to control their emotions and themselves.

A sober and practical mind helped Alina deal with different types of clients and hold a conversation without affectation. But she preferred the scruffy and inexperienced ones. She poured her heart into them, sometimes barely restraining herself: she so wanted to drive them mad with her caresses. As they sensed this preferential treatment, they maintained a certain level of commitment to her. She glowed and smiled sweetly, charming dimples in her cheeks, disarming visitors with her genuine innocence. She seemed to dissolve in every-

---

[36] A water seeker is an allegory of a poet endowed with an instinct that is prophetically blind. See, for example, a poem by Fyodor Tyutchev, a Russian poet: *To others, nature has given a prophetically blind instinct — with it they hear the waters even in the earth's dark depths.*

one, unaware that these lucky ones would repeat her name in their lustful dreams.

A gloomy, lanky young man with a pale face once confessed that he set money aside from every paycheck to go to the Club at least once every couple of months.

"This is the only reason for my existence! It's like a fairy tale here! And you are a fairy!"

During the session he transformed; rolling his Adam's apple, he muttered lustfully:

"You have an incredible, endless body."

Sliding his lips over the delicate skin, he covered her shoulders and chest with passionate kisses, constantly swallowing saliva.

An elderly, clean-shaven man with a mole by his right nostril said he was glad the USSR had collapsed and shared his sorrow at the fact that his time for sensual pleasures was gone.

"Oh, what a waste of my youth! *Life has flown by in vain*," stroking his sweaty bald head, he added with a look of regret.

"You can make up for it now. Wait, don't tear your shirt! What are you doing?!" Alina exclaimed playfully and helped the client undress.

The old man appreciated the girl's resourcefulness and leaned into her breasts. After a while he lay down on the bed and plunged into bliss of the girl's touch.

"Oh my dear! You gave me energy! Very sweet!" he mumbled cheerfully as a goodbye.

She never forgot to ask for a tip.

Another time, a gnarled man with a tough face persistently demanded intercourse.

"Are you crazy?! Get your paws off me! What a clown!" Alina was outraged and immediately called security. She sat on the edge of the bed trembling in fear for a long time.

One day, a young man caressed her earlobes, and Alina accidentally fell asleep. Holding his breath, he tenderly examined her tired angelic face in every detail, watching her eyes move anxiously under her closed eyelids. He noticed a tiny bit of mascara fall from her eyelashes into the crescent-shaped dimple on her cheek.

Like pollen from a flower, thought the young man. His gaze wandered over the girl's body, as if in front of him was a divine nude posing for the painting "The Origin of the World".[37] He sat motionless for half an hour, hopelessly trying to transport himself into the girl's dream. Then he carefully dressed and went out into the corridor. He asked the Queen to neither wake Alina nor to punish her and paid extra for the visit.

One client, about fifty years old, with a mustache and a bald head, was stroking Alina's legs when she suddenly felt cold metal: the titanium plates were still inside her graceful shins. A sharp pain ran along her ankles, her calves cramped, and tears appeared in her eyes.

What a fragile girl, the visitor thought, raising his heavy eyebrows in surprise; looking closer, he noticed the neat scars on her legs. Figuring out the situation, he recommended Alina not delay the removal of the plates and gave her money for the surgery. It turned out that he was a doctor.

Alina followed his advice: she took time off school and work and went to the hospital. The surgeon removed the titanium plates, but had to leave one screw, since its head got twisted off.

After the surgery, Alina was put in a shared room, where she heard the quiet groans of patients at night. A very young woman lay on the next bed; she was covered in plaster casts for multiple fractures. The next morning Alina listened carefully to her sad story. The woman's boyfriend had left her. She didn't know how to continue to live with that loss, and jumped from a fourth floor balcony.

Alina listened in silence, thinking she would never injure or kill herself of her own free will. And she thought about how one absurd tragic accident ended the life of her beloved Yurik. She continued to be affected by that accident: here she was again in the hospital, one screw left in her leg, likely to stay, and she had no strength to get out of this vortex of fate.

---

[37] A picture painted by the French artist Gustave Courbet in 1866.

She remembered Yurik and recalled the evening when they became close in an irresistible whirlwind of passion. Alina went into the carpentry workshop, where Yurik worked alone until late that night. Dressed in an A-shirt and loose trousers, with his legs spread wide for balance, he deftly wielded a carpenter's plane: thin, resin-smelling pine shavings curled from under it. The floor was covered with a layer of soft shavings. Yurik turned around, put the plane aside, and timidly came up to her. Alina felt light-headed as his hands gently wrapped her slender waist. And suddenly the world sweetly and blissfully turned upside down.

Alina burst into silent tears at the foot of the bed of her unfortunate roommate, not sure if it was sympathy for the woman's grief or for her own. Then she shut her eyes, wet with tears, and, burying herself in the blanket, lay there until dinner was served.

Two weeks later, the sutures were removed, and she was discharged.

Working at the Club attracted Alina. She could communicate with men there and receive compliments and affection from them without subsequently paying with humiliation and loss of independence. She often admitted to herself that she liked it when people looked at her naked body. Almost everything in the Club operated according to protocol, and this "almost" both held her back and attracted her with its uncertainty. But such service to restrained sensuality took a lot of effort and time, and she had to petition the university to switch to distance learning.

One day in early September, she was chosen by a man of about forty-five, pleasant in appearance and with an innocent face. He introduced himself as Ruslan.

He resembles Nikolai Baskov[38] a bit, Alina thought.

They went into the far room without windows. There was a tiny shower in the corner, a wide bed with intricate baroque curlicues on the headboard, and a table made of thick glass

---

[38] Nikolai V. Baskov is a popular Russian tenor singer.

next to it. Muted violet light illuminated the room, whose walls were covered with purple wallpaper printed with fantastic flowers.

"Familiar pattern. Like my aunt's apartment in Ghelendzhik," Ruslan mentioned.

To get to know each other, they drank champagne and toasted to their mutual health.

"Would you like to smoke a hookah?" Alina asked.

Ruslan shook his head.

Alina untied and casually threw off her wispy robe. Ruslan swung forward and, hugging the girl awkwardly, threw her onto the bed, hitting the tabletop with his foot. One glass crashed to the floor and broke.

"No problem. It happens," Alina said, getting up, and began collecting the fragments.

"Do not get distracted. You can bring the mop in later, okay?" Ruslan said with a guilty smile.

Alina performed a relaxing massage artistically. She sat with her bare thighs on the client's buttocks and, accompanied by meditative music, rubbed coconut oil on his back with a light touch. Ruslan's heart began to beat rapidly.

The silence did not last long. At first they talked about the weather and cars. Alina casually mentioned her village. She said that she was studying to get a degree and dreamed of becoming a makeup artist. She wanted to travel some day. After all, she had never ventured outside the region.

Ruslan listened absentmindedly, saying every now and then that she had all her life ahead of her and everything would work out just fine. Sometimes he would ask her something and immediately forget the answer. Then he suddenly said:

"I am starving for love!"

"Intercourse is forbidden... So is kissing on the lips!" Alina shook her head sharply, and her hair fell like a silk avalanche onto Ruslan's wet back.

"You do not understand," he said, irritated, and buried his face in the pillow. "I want big, true love! To suffer from passion! To languish! And to be moved by her, to melt!"

"They say if you cleanse your soul, true love will come," Alina tried to calm the client down.

She asked Ruslan to turn over on his back. Soon his scrotum and shaft were in her soft hands. The man started breathing rapidly and groaned. After three minutes the session ended with his complete relaxation: a happy ending, as they said in the Club.

Ruslan lay serenely with a blurred gaze, and the tattoo of a grinning tiger on his sculpted chest rose and fell with his breathing.

Alina took a napkin and wiped the semen off her palm. Then, like lovers, they went into the shower. Lowering his eyelids, Ruslan stood still under the stream of water, enjoying the perfection and smoothness of the girl's body...

Two hours passed in the blink of an eye.

Ruslan dressed silently, looked around the room for the last time and followed the girl into the corridor, feeling a wonderful lightness throughout his body, as if he was flying. He felt as if the carpet was swaying slightly under his feet. The Queen tiptoed out of the last room and, holding out the Club discount card, asked if everything had gone well. Next to these shining women, Ruslan seemed somewhat gloomy. He muttered some words of gratitude and timidly promised to visit again. He found his newly purchased cap in the closet by the exit and graciously said goodbye. Opening the door slightly, he slipped sideways outside. After walking a few steps down the street, he turned back into Konstantin, or simply Kostya.

Earlier, while Kostya was at the Club, a rain shower filled the air with moisture. Wind rustled, shaking the wet tree tops. Rainwater flowed rapidly along the roadside, and gurgling and foaming, rushed through the sewer grates. Rare drops fell from the crowns of tall poplars, and their fall made the roadside grass quiver.

Waiting for the tram, Kostya stood under a birch tree.

I won't go there again! All this is a mirage! It is a glimpse of twilight obsession. A pathetic **copy of something that doesn't exist**[39]... *Yes, there is more truth in this birch tree than in that entire venue,* he thought and put his palm on the bleached trunk of the birch. Then he said quietly:

---

[39] A simulacrum.

"I feel the urge to press the naked breasts of the birch to my body..."[40]

A breeze blew, and the wet leaves of the birch tree, fluttering, touched Kostya's face. Smiling widely, he looked around with the enlightened gaze of a newly born man.

An older woman was lightly walking towards him along the sidewalk, pulling a heavy bag on wheels. Two boys stopped at the crossing near the school. One blurted out something with a sly grin, nodding his head towards the Club. The other one looked at his mate and laughed.

"Whelps," Kostya said in a low voice, so as not to be heard.

He felt uneasy, as if he had recently done something forbidden.

She is a cheerful girl, although not very bright. And why the hell was she asking about cars? A simple thing like her! he thought, chewing a randomly picked birch leaf. *She could have become my inspiration... in a different situation, of course! But bless her heart! Let her entertain others!*

A half-empty red tram Number Five[41] came rumbling along. Kostya nimbly jumped onto the step. He gave the conductor exact change for the ticket and, walking forward through the cabin, as if by chance sat next to a girl with brightly painted full lips. Her sharp knees peeked out from under her fashionable handbag. Her gaze down under her long eyelashes, she moved her elegant finger across the iPhone screen in deep concentration, scrolling through the news feed and smiling at something.

Meanwhile, the street outside the window rolled out, slowing down at the stops and accelerating after the expected jerk

---

[40] A quote from a poem by Sergei A. Yesenin, a notable Russian poet; translation by Roger Pulvers, an Australian playwright, theater director, translator and filmmaker.

[41] An allusion to the Russian song *Tram No 5* by Michail Andreev; Andreev wrote the song for a Russian patriotic rock band Lyube: *...Hey, lovely girls, we have not lived our lives in vain. Take me, tram number 5 to Cheryomushki, take me, old lovely fiver, there! Take me there!* (translation by Sergei Kolesov).

and dull clang, as if intending to catch up with the post-storm cloud which smothered the calm setting sun.

Kostya considered talking to the girl beside him. But he felt frustrated, not knowing where to start. He wanted to ask her name: was it Rose, Isabella, or Margarita? He felt as if they weren't riding in a tram, but sitting next to each other on the wide seat of a luxury limo. Throwing an indecisive glance at her clenched knees, he gritted his teeth and jumped off at the next stop near the city park.

Squaring his shoulders and greedily inhaling the humid air, he slowly walked along the wide alley through the clouds of steam rising from the damp asphalt spotted with occasional mirrors of puddles. The sapphire bubbles of street lamps were already burning through their foggy halos, illuminating with their miserable light the geometrically correct flower beds of marigolds and brassica. There were empty wet benches along the road. In the distance, a Devil's wheel loomed like a vague dotted line above the clumps of trees. On the other side of the park, at the intersection, Kostya noticed a florist kiosk, and involuntarily thought: *When was the last time I gave flowers to a woman?*

Later that evening, he returned to his small apartment on the fifth floor, crammed with books and stacks of paper. He wrote about the day's adventure in his journal. Was that at all surprising? He loved journaling. Sometimes he sat under the cozy green shade of the table lamp, re-reading his notes, reliving past events. Sometimes that would give rise to new thoughts. The day's events were a special case: for the first time he touched a woman whom he did not love. And just recently he had dreams that he would be caressed by his beloved.

He recalled the days of deep disappointment and unrealistic hopes.

He was married once. His wife thought him a genius; but after three years of intimacy, she left for someone else without giving him a child. Kostya, however, did not stop believing in his exclusivity and special purpose, and suffered because he had not yet passed his precious genes on to anyone. Raised on Russian literature, he hated insincerity and, suspecting fraud in every smile, avoided people. However, occasionally, he did want to have a heart-to-heart talk with someone!

There were thick notebooks on the bookshelf next to Nabokov, with a crumpled yellowed piece of paper sticking out of one; it was his spermogram. Kostya opened the journal to the bookmarked page and, plopping down on the sofa, plunged into reading his entries from twenty years ago.

*Or should I tell love to go to hell? Maybe it's time to move on to **the erotic of the highest rank**[42]?* he thought as he sluggishly undressed and went to bed. *But tomorrow, tomorrow...*

One morning, Kostya went for a jog in a nearby forested park on the southern outskirts of the city. The path along which he jogged meandered through a pine forest and was covered with pine needles. Sometimes it broke out onto a high bank where a wide river shimmered in the rays of the sun below, revealing countless pebble rifts.

The river has become so shallow! Why haven't I noticed it before? Kostya thought, slowing down on the steep cliff.

At home, the first thing he did was wash off the stifling sweat; then he rubbed himself dry vigorously with a shaggy towel and paused for a second in front of the bathroom mirror: fine wrinkles were obvious in the corners of his eyes.

That's all right! he mentally cheered himself and winked. *I should remove the tattoo, though.*

For the past three years, Kostya had worked remotely, at home on the computer, and he had distanced himself from society. His workday dragged by slowly and monotonously in the oppressive stuffiness of the city, and that night Kostya dreamed of a full-flowing river behind the forested park, at his regular jogging spot.

A white pleasure boat was moving up the river, and its deck was crowded. Couples waltzed leisurely and monotonously to a loud tune.

---

[42] A quote from Nikolai A. Berdyaev's work *The Russian Idea* (1946).

It was me who made this river navigable, Kostya thought proudly, standing at the edge of the steep cliff. Then he stepped forward and, spreading his arms wide, fell down. The terror of the fall gave way to delight when he confidently and triumphantly flew over the abyss towards the ship. He recognized himself as one of the dancers.

"Where are we going?" he asked the lady waltzing with him. "There is a shoal over there! The work is not finished yet!"

"Nonsense! The captain knows best," she answered carefree, fixing admiring green eyes on him. She was wearing a short transparent black silk dress, and nothing under it. Before they had time to make a few steps, a strong grinding sound was heard. The deck tilted sharply.

"Hold on to my hair!" shouted the strange girl.

Kostya grabbed the girl by her thin waist with his left hand, wrapped the soft ringlets of her hair around the fingers of his right, and forcefully pulled her towards him. The next moment a wave of excitement ran down his spine. He planted a frantic kiss on her hot lips and took her as the climax of his passion erupted on a flotation ring, torn from the board by someone in the general turmoil. She moaned, and suddenly wings grew from her shoulders. Together they skyrocketed and flew like a shadow over the muddy water, away from the boat that ran aground. The remaining couples squirmed and floundered madly on the tilted deck: a total orgy was on.

I hope she's at least sixteen. However, it doesn't matter anymore. This must be a dream! A fairy tale, likely! having exhausted all his strength, Kostya thought feverishly. During the flight, a wave of bliss engulfed him. They began to move away from the Earth. It became difficult to breathe in the low-density atmosphere, and he woke up.

Wow! To dream of such things! he stammered sleepily, feeling a sticky spot on the crumpled sheet. He lay there feeling overwhelmed, for five minutes, trying to remember the stranger's face. It was eclectic; or rather it changed constantly. First, the features of the girl he noticed on the tram the other day arose in his memory, and then it resembled Alina's face,

after—his ex-wife's: she was so distant, and he forgot her already, but her portrait still stood on his desk, reminding him of their break up and his internal split. Finally, in a flurry of these faces, the face of his dear mother appeared, as if in a photo from a family album. She stood there, so very young in a white robe, squinting in the bright sun, on the deck of a diesel boat, next to a fire shield and a flotation ring with the inscription "Health" on it. Her blonde hair fluttered in the wind, framing a charming smile on her wide face. There was something angelic in her appearance. Kostya recalled a family legend that he was conceived on board of a floating clinic, where his future mother worked over the summer. This happened almost near the Arctic Circle, where dwarf birch grew along the banks of rivers. Was it even imaginable?

He sat down on the edge of the bed, shivering from a slight chill. He shook off his dreams and reluctantly stood up, cracked his joints while walking, went to the window, and watched the blue-gray sky through the dusty, long-unwashed glass for a long time, looking at the place where the crowns of old poplars intertwined. He stood there forever, as if he had lost his connection to the world, and suddenly and unexpectedly thought about death, its inevitability...

Coward! This is too much! I'm no longer a little boy! It's time to change my attitude to life and fill it with meaning, he finally decided. *Otherwise, as the Michurinians[43] say, I will turn into a seed. I cannot man the barricades; that's not an option... Ridiculous!*

Kostya returned to the desk and resolutely opened the laptop to compose the text of the advertisement. He instantly found the right words: *I don't need to think hard here, the blood type, as they say, is "on your sleeve," and personal feelings in this matter play a secondary role.* At the end he added: *"Together we will build a nation of healthy people."* He ended up deleting the line: it was too pretentious; it did not match the overall style.

Alina bought a small, cozy studio in a new neighborhood. She continued to work at the Club; she could neither see herself living without a man's touch nor engaging in a close relationship. Sometimes, at night, she was overcome by a deep melancholy and an awareness of the brevity of human life. At these moments, she thought that she had lost all her inherent motherly love and tenderness at the Club. The thought that she could never be loved again would not leave her mind. But

---

[43] Michurinians are followers of Ivan V. Michurin, a Russian practitioner of natural selection to produce new types of crop plants.

Alina did not want to make any promises or commitments. She remembered how painful it was to witness the constant fighting of her parents. And jealous fighting would be inevitable because of her line of work!

She adopted a black cat from a shelter. At night, it lay on her chest and kneaded with its paws contentedly.

"You are my little tiger," she whispered, falling asleep. And the cat stretched and purred.

It seemed that life may have improved: she had a job and her own home. But for some reason, Alina was anxious more and more about her future.

One evening, when the sunset was already disappearing in crimson clouds, she was walking along the streets of the city and found herself in front of the window of the flower shop where she used to work as a college freshman. Afraid of running into the familiar saleswoman and being questioned, she cast a wary eye through the glass at the pavilion filled with Dutch roses, multi-colored tulips, amazing lilies, delicate callas, and carnations. A young man was choosing flowers. Following the movement of his pointing hand, the saleswoman lifted the stems; water dripped from them.

That night Alina had a dream in which she forgot her name (they called her Rose at the Club). Limping, she walked through a damp, dark tunnel, and there was no end to it. The walls were covered with red-brown mold, and pearly mucus hung from the stone vaults. She could hear water dripping. She heard heels clicking and echoing; a child's laughter came from somewhere. It became difficult to breathe. It seemed like there would never be sunshine again. The tunnel suddenly turned into a long, deserted corridor. A naked, half-bent figure appeared in one of the side doors. The man shook his hand in front of him in a "wait a second!" gesture. But as soon as Alina got closer, his fingers turned into terrible pincers. Alina recoiled and, overcoming the dream pain in her shin, ran as fast as she could. She spotted the Queen in the vague depths of an open room; the woman was smoking a long hookah and making flirty faces.

Finally, the corridor curved and dead-ended; it was the place where a mirror used to hang at the Club. A girl with a face pale as white marble, like the Madonna from a Renaissance painting, stood against the wall. She wore an azure garment and seemed to glow from the inside.

"This is a men's club! What do you want here?" Alina mumbled in confusion.

"I am your client's future bride," the strange girl said calmly.

"Which client? We have lots of them! They know me, but I'm not supposed to know them. Pick one!" Alina spoke defensively, but with more confidence. "What is your name?"

"Love. Love for people..." The stranger said and disappeared in a flash of light.

Alina, trembling with anxiety, saw her reflection in the shards of the broken mirror.

The next morning, she had bad period cramps, and dark circles lay under her eyes. She did not go to the Club. Tucking her legs under and throwing her mother's blanket over her shoulders, she settled on the sofa with her laptop to watch a silly TV show about the afterlife. Afterwards, she surfed the Internet for dating ads. One ad caught her attention:

I will help you conceive healthy and beautiful children. A few facts about me: I am 45 years old, 6 ft tall, 180 lbs, Slavic in appearance, with gray-blue eyes and blond hair; blood type A+, good genetic background, no bad habits, no health problems. I work out. There are superagers in my family. I am of noble Russian blood. I have a university degree and a high level of intelligence, as well as diverse talents. I am reasonable, calm, non conflicting, and kind. I am ready to provide a certificate of being STD free and a perfect spermogram. Konstantin

They agreed to meet next to the wooden fortress that had been rebuilt at the original site of the city.

Will he bring flowers to our first date? Alina wondered.

She left the Club at dawn. Day was breaking, and the fortress tower with its observation deck was already illuminated by the

first rays of
the sun.

The work shift
had been difficult.
The clients came and
went like ghosts. First,
there was a sleek, pot-bellied man with small eyes and bushy
eyebrows. He lounged in a leather chair demanding the best
girl. Although his gaze settled on Alina, it was clear that he did
not trust his first impression. "Is she a master? A real master?"
he frantically asked the Queen in a breaking voice in front of
Alina.

"You are as tough as a diamond!" Alina said, diligently mas-
saging the flabby flesh of the visitor.

"What a delight! What ecstasy!" he muttered. Afterwards, he
spoke sincerely about women's fate, spiritual well being, and
Mother Russia, in an unctuous, sing-song voice.

Alina asked if he wanted to stay for another hour. She was
eager to listen to his beautiful, chaste words, to learn something deep. But the man refused; he did, however, mention
that he personally knew the Governor.

Another client came in with disheveled hair, his right eye-
lid was twitching nervously, his eyes watering. He began with
a confession: he and his wife had had a fight and he decided to
spend the night elsewhere. Such visitors were common in the
Club, but this one was clearly in a state of panic. He examined
the room to see if there were video cameras installed somewhere, and during the massage he squirmed hysterically, tick-

lish. He complained about a bunch of things under his breath. The poor fellow calmed down only at the very end, when, with a quiet sigh of relief, he lay peacefully for several minutes. Later, he pulled on his pants and shoved his sky-blue underwear in his pocket. Standing up straight, he cast a cold, arrogant gaze at Alina.

It was well past midnight when the last client left, and the young women were free to go. The sleepy Queen peeked out of her room, holding a glossy magazine with a Chinese fan stuck between its pages, under her arm. She stopped Alina and shared the news that she would be resigning soon, and asked Alina to take her place.

"You, my girl, have a talent and a good reputation as a master; you know the job; you can recruit your own staff. In time, you will turn into an excellent administrator with a good salary. Think about your future. You will have to stop loving someday," she said in lieu of a goodbye and left, humming a sweet tune.

The offer was very tempting.

Well, I can be a Queen soon! Alina thought as she left the Club. But she immediately shuddered at the thought: that was not how she had envisioned her future.

Alina walked, rapturously inhaling the air: it was still cool after the night, with the intangible smell of chokecherry blossoms. She heard the monotonous croaking of frogs in the backwater. But some mysterious growing noise was gradually overcoming every other sound.

In a daze, the girl froze at an empty intersection, anxiously awaiting the appearance of the unknown object. Suddenly, a sweeper truck appeared from around the corner. A huge, dusty brush rotated in its underbelly, shuffling unpleasantly: whoosh! whoosh! whoosh!

Five minutes passed before Alina woke up from her stupor. By that time, the sweeper had already disappeared into the wavering distance of Mir Avenue. The street fell silent for a moment, and she could hear a roadside poplar rustling its dusty leaves.

There was only one day left before the appointed date. She needed to rest, recover, and call her mother: Mother always waited for her daughter to call, and every call made Mother very happy.

A black cab was driving by. Alina stepped to the edge of the pavement, raised her hand and called: "Taxi! Taxi!"

From a distance, a lone bespectacled balding man watched a beautiful girl hail a taxi; a pigeon fluttered from under the wheels of the vehicle. The girl ducked to get into the car, and her dangling earrings glittered and danced on her earlobes.

The man smiled, amazed: it had been at least twenty years since the last time somebody in the city caught a taxi so casually and innocently. Hardly imaginable!

Alina gave the driver the address, and glanced out of the window, noticing a lone man under the canopy of a tram stop; he was gazing dreamily into the distance.

The car picked up speed. Buildings, trees, thickets of flowering chokecherry, signs on storefronts, billboards, the gloss of shop windows, and rare early passers-by flashed outside the window. A thin feral dog ran along the sidewalk limping and favoring a hind leg. The bell tower dome floated majestically in the distance.

Everything she saw was familiar to Alina, but, like a screen, it hid that elusive thing that caused her melancholy and anxiety. She didn't want to know the reasons, at least not at the moment.

"Don't worry; I'll take you where you need to go. I know the Emerald Hills district. There used to be a birch grove there," the driver turned to Alina and, noticing the sadness in the girl's eyes, grinned. The lines of his wrinkled, ugly face immediately smoothed out, as if he had taken off a terrible mask.

The corners of Alina's glossed lips turned up in a smile, but she remained silent, looking into the distance with a mysterious gaze. The breeze flowing from the window rolled down halfway moved a blond strand of hair on her temple. She suddenly realized that she would never return to the Club. She knew that her life had taken a wrong turn somewhere, but she could still fix it. And the fix was simple: in a few minutes she would come home, take off her clothes, and get into the shower. Then she would pick up the phone and call her mother, maybe she would cry, and beg to be forgiven for not having visited for a long time. And the next day a new, interesting life would begin.

OLD FORD, NEW TENANT

It was nearly noon, but for me this spring day did not have any chance of making sense. I was puttering around the laboratory; my brain refused to work; I felt some sort of mirthless void. *I urgently need coffee, to perk up, and start looking at things positively,* I decided.

The BSL2[44] is not very serious, but no beverages are allowed in the lab. I took the thermos, went out into the courtyard of the Research Center and headed towards a small artificial pond.

Just a month ago, I finally discovered a pattern in the relationship between the size of morpho-functional blocks of a growing embryo and the Gordon wavelength of differentiation. However, last Monday the group leader unexpectedly announced the imminent closure of our laboratory: we had funds to cover only four months of research. In this situation, looking for a new job would not be such a stupid thing to do. What to do with the unpublished research results? After all, this is a real breakthrough in science! However, seeking a job and writing an article at the same time seemed to be beyond my capabilities.

I told Anfisa, an old friend from another department, about the upcoming layoff.

"The United States should not support Ukraine!" she said, non sequitur.

My jaw dropped.

"The boss said the grant was not renewed. In the past ten years, this has often happened in the USA. Over the years, one third of all laboratories in our Center have closed. You know

---

[44] Biological Safety Grade 2.

this as well as I do," I began, but gave up, recognizing the fighting mood of my vis-a-vis.

I did not feel like continuing this conversation; and to think that once upon a time we used to listen to Bulat Okudzhava[45] together! The circle of friends was already shrinking like a piece of shagreen leather. I could count the remaining ones on the fingers of one hand. "I try to live in peace with my conscience," Anfisa sometimes said when our opinions differed.

I came to the pond; fog was rising off its surface. This pond never froze in the winter; apparently, there were warm springs somewhere nearby, so it was a favorite hangout for ducks year round. Indeed, a pair of birds swam out from the prominent stems of last year's withered cattail and headed for the shore, begging for food. I set the thermos on the table, patted my empty pockets and spread my arms to show the ducks that I had nothing to give them.

Sitting down on the cold metal bench was not an attractive option. I watched the surface of the water and reflections of the willows leaning over the pond on the opposite shore. There was typical Montana scenery behind them: white peaks of a mountain range, framed by blue sky.

I admired the magnificent landscape, but even that did not improve my gloomy mood that bordered on desperation. There was another reason for this: the boss asked me earlier that morning if everything was okay. *Obviously, he shows increased attention to his staff. You never know what someone could do after such unpleasant news,* I thought at first.

"You don't sleep at home, do you? Do you sleep in the car?" he elaborated.

I just stared at him.

"There is a sleeping bag in your car, and clothes."

Some homeless person must have gotten into my old Ford, since the doors don't lock, I thought. The car had run reliably for over thirty years, but in the past year the transmission be-

---

[45] Bulat S. Okudzhava was a Soviet and Russian poet, writer, musician, novelist, and singer-songwriter.

gan to act out. I had no parking space at my house, so I parked the Ford at the Center over the winter. You never know. Frugality became my second nature, what with having lived in Russia.

I didn't want to go checking on the Ford. Delaying the inevitable, I stood at the edge of the water and took small sips of coffee from my thermos. Finally, after the last sip, I slowly walked to the parking lot. I came to the car and peered in through the dirty window. My fears were confirmed: someone's sleeping bag was spread out on the back seat. Carefully opening the door, I checked the bag: it was empty. I sighed with relief: *Thank God, no one is in there. What if I found a frozen corpse? It's cold at night: get drunk, fall asleep and that would be the last that you were ever seen! And I would have to answer stupid questions from the police. How would I prove that I had nothing to do with it?*

There were somebody's belongings in the car: clothes, a radio, some bottles, and several cans of food. I sniffed the air inside: the smell was quite bearable, no hint of mustiness. I closed the door, looked around; I was alone.

Well, so be it. He can live here. I don't care. It's good that my car is useful to someone and became a shelter in difficult times, so I decided in the spirit of charity. The number of homeless people in the city had increased noticeably during and after the COVID pandemic.

I returned to the lab, hoping to concentrate on my work. Yet, I was curious. Every day I went to the car and looked inside: no one was there. To go there late at night or early in the morning to surely catch the new tenants of the old Ford was not what I really wanted to do.

Finally, the following week, I saw a purple knitted hat flash in the shallow ditch just outside the parking lot. I came closer and yelled:

"Hi! "

The person stood up, brushed themselves off, and raised their head. It was a middle-aged woman with a puffy face of a drunk, in blue jeans and a shabby jacket. She was holding something in her hand, maybe a notebook. *She is an alcoholic,* I figured out. *Go figure!* I asked:

"Are those your things in my car?"

"Yes," she answered in a hoarse voice. Her blue eyes struck me with their calmness and depth.

"I understand. Hard times can happen to anyone," I continued.

"I have an attorney," she said warily, but with perfect confidence, and compressed her thin lips.

I spoke English with a strong accent, and the inevitable question was not long in coming:

"Are you Russian?"

"Yes, but I don't support the war in Ukraine," I said hastily. "Unheard evil! Joe Biden is great, he immediately saw right through Putin."

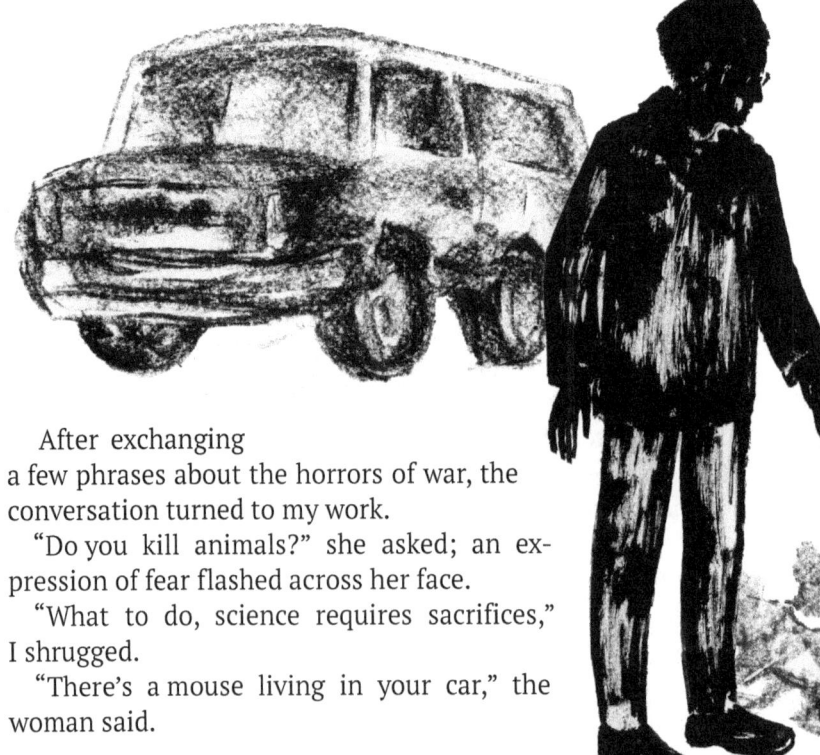

After exchanging a few phrases about the horrors of war, the conversation turned to my work.

"Do you kill animals?" she asked; an expression of fear flashed across her face.

"What to do, science requires sacrifices," I shrugged.

"There's a mouse living in your car," the woman said.

"Does it bother you at night?"

"It makes some noise, but I sleep tight."

"Last year, a mouse lived in the trunk, too," I smiled. "And yellow jackets made a nest in a rearview mirror in the summer. One day, a rabbit ran under the car in a parking lot and managed to get stuck there somehow. Fortunately, it got home safely with me, and then ran away. Are you a new tenant?"

Was this how the conversation really went? I am not sure; I didn't speak English very well. The technical terms were the most difficult to remember. I actively gestured and pointed my finger, trying to explain that the wasps' nest was not in the rearview mirror, but right behind it: in the housing where the mirror's rotating mechanism is located. The woman nodded and watched my gestures in bewilderment.

We talked more about our love of animals. The expression on Greta's face — that was her name — changed quickly, switching from brightness to melancholy, which I mistook for calmness due to my inexperience at first. I realized that she had a receptive nature with an exaggerated sense of fairness. She told me about trivial things, winding a strand of her blond hair around her finger. It turned out that Greta used to have a parrot, but it flew away.

I listened to her, intrigued, and thought: *She used to be a pretty woman.* If I had known then that I would be writing about this encounter, I would have definitely asked her how long she had been homeless and what she had done for a living before. But on that day my compassion for her prevailed, apparently. Anyway, who would reveal all their secrets to a stranger? I didn't tell her that I might soon become unemployed, too.

"If you have nowhere to stay, you can live in the Ford for a maximum of two weeks. I have to move the car at the end of April."

"Okay," she replied with a smile.

A woman with no specific occupation, an apparent alcoholic, climbed into my car, and I, who had never given money to a single homeless person before, neither in Russia nor in the States, apologized to her for being Russian and for killing poor animals for science. I returned to the laboratory.

"How are things at work?" my wife asked when I was back home, tired, at the end of the day.

"Well, not too bad," I answered vaguely.

"Are you looking for a new job?"

"Yes, I am," I lied and did not mention the homeless woman living in my old car.

At night I tossed and turned in bed, worrying that Greta was freezing or starving. I imagined her, wrapped in a blanket, looking in the rearview mirror, straightening her hair... *If I lived in a car myself, I'd hang curtains,* I thought, finally falling asleep.

The next day was cloudless. My depressing mood dissipated, and I actively began writing the scientific article, almost forgetting about my old Ford and its tenant. And no wonder! After all, I always left my new Toyota in front of the entrance to the Research Center, without going into the main parking lot. I should also add that my passion for science had been saving me from such noble impulses of my soul throughout my life.

Two weeks later, chokecherry trees bloomed between the duck pond and the back parking lot. The luxuriant white tops were visible from the lab window. Looking out the window once again, I remembered my Ford and immediately jumped up and ran outside. I inhaled the chokecherry smell, as if that was the reason why I had left the laboratory. Then, I went to the abandoned car. The woman's belongings were still there.

Maybe everything will resolve itself. After all, she promised to move out, I thought with prelapsarian naivety, drunk on spring air.

At a scientific seminar, Anfisa said to me:

"They say you are running a homeless shelter. How much do you get paid? Are you sleeping with this woman?" she quipped.

"Nothing of the sort! Who told you that?" I responded defensively.

Anfisa caught me off guard. *I hope these rumors don't reach my wife; they can also ruin my professional references, and then I won't get a new job. It's time to be done with this charity. What a dreamer I have been!* I was annoyed with myself. I felt regret for a moment that I had not asked for the phone number of my tenant. It would have been nice to warn her; I didn't feel like throwing her stuff into the trash.

There was nothing else to be done. That same day, I carefully rolled up Greta's sleeping bag and placed it under the nearest juniper bush. *However, I could have told her right away to get out immediately. Since I didn't say it, it means I am not heartless like others...* ***I gave an onion to the hungry***,[46] I thought, scooping out her things with disgust. Then I charged the car battery, managed to start the car, and drove it to a car dealership to sell for parts. First, I unscrewed the license plate. I knew a place where this plate could be useful. When the war will end, I will go to my home town in Siberia. When I visited a couple of years ago, there was a pub where license plates from all over the world decorated the walls. It felt like a hundred years had passed, but I promised the owner of that establishment to bring a rare object from abroad: a license plate from a Montana car.

At the end of June, I was laid off. I received unemployment benefits for the next three months and deposited weekly checks into the family account. It was a great time for recreation, better than a vacation. Lots of free time! During this time, I read a dozen books; I am so fond of literature! In my youth, I imagined fantastic stories about Sepulkas,[47] and later wrote stories about my life. Now I had no idea what was true and what was fiction. Surprisingly, we did not care about

---

[46] An allusion to *The Brothers Karamazov*, the last novel by Fyodor Dostoevsky, a Russian writer..

[47] Fictional objects found in several works by Stanisław Lem, a Polish writer of science fiction and essays.

politics during these three months at all! My wife and I even went to the beach by the ocean for a short while. Unfortunately, nobody can receive unemployment checks forever. I didn't want to leave Montana: it was one of only a few states in America with clean air and amazing nature.

In October I finally got a job at the department that studied plants. Now I was researching the development of a new barley that could be grown outside of a greenhouse. I hoped this would be the capstone of my career.

Sometimes I thought of my tenant. Did she need help? It would be interesting to ask what she thought about the Gaza Strip.

But today I couldn't take it anymore. I surrendered to temptation. I collected some bread crumbs from the table and drove to my previous place of work. It was Saturday, and I thought that I could at least feed the ducks.

I arrived only to discover that the duck pond was gone. Did they fill it in with dirt? Not believing my eyes, I walked twice and then three times around the place where the pond had been only six months ago; but there was only a flat lawn dusted with snow.

I stood there, ruffled up like a sparrow — the poorest bird ever — and pecked at the breadcrumbs in my palm. Then I stared into the distance for a long time, watching the cold peaks of the mountain range, and suddenly I felt the reality slipping away irreversibly with unbearable speed. *Existence mine... Life of mine,* I chuckled to myself. What is there to be done? I took a notebook out of my pocket and wrote: "*It was nearly noon, but...*"

Can I expand it to ten thousand characters with spaces at least, to capture a few of these moments? Just for fun and my love for humankind?

GOLDEN DUST

A heavy ruby bee
Flies home with its fragrant load,
And its slow body turns purple
In the raw clouds of the west.[48]

Georgy Shengeli

Many years ago, I happened to meet a Mr. Vilen Zhukov. Everyone called him Willy. We worked in adjacent laboratories at the Institute of Morphogenesis in one of the Siberian cities. After Perestroika, Willy left the city of his ancestors and moved to Montana, USA, where he continued to pursue science, and where he kept bees as a hobby. We hadn't seen each other for a long time, so last year in May, after a conference in Seattle, I dropped in to visit Willy. He was pleased to host me at his house on the outskirts of Bozeman, a small college town located thirty miles from the source of the Missouri River.

We had tea on the large porch with a beautiful view of the Rocky Mountains. Their peaks were snowcapped. There was no fence around the house, and the neatly trimmed lawn flowed into a blooming meadow. The meadow sloped down into the valley, where the Gallatin River, one of the three tributaries of the Missouri, glittered like a narrow silver ribbon. A soft buzz of bees filled the air. I went to the edge of the terrace, put my hands on the railing and said enviously:

"You're settled here just like Martin Heidegger. You are refining your ideas in the midst of a mountain landscape."

"My ideas have long been dedicated to farming activities," said Willy, stretching in a sling-chair.

---

[48] A quote from the poem *Sickles* by Georgy A. Shengeli.

"I don't see any farmsteads," I said, glancing over the valley once again.

"I keep bees, man!" Willy pointed to the colorful beehives next to the house under the lindens. "They fly to the river. Now, the nectar comes from mixed flowers, until the neighbor's alfalfa blossoms. This year, I want to buy a Russian honeybee queen as an experiment."

"Why Russian?" I interrupted him impatiently and put a piece of cheesecake on my plate.

"Russian honey bees are highly valued in the US!" Willy tossed his arms up in the air. "They are resistant to adverse environments, though they are quite aggressive," Willy quickly stood up and added some hot water from the Tula samovar into the mugs.

"As far as I remember, John Steinbeck mentioned in his Russian Journal one state-owned farm beekeeper who admired queen bees from California, and he believed that American honey bees were resistant to freezing." I knew the books quite well, so I could bring up quotes *ad hoc*.

"Maybe those were the ones bred for export?" Willy smiled widely.

I replied:

"Ha-ha! You haven't lost your sense of humor after all! I recognize my long-time friend!"

The next day, Willy invited me to head over to the village of Pony to the hot spring. A couple of miles before Pony, we turned onto a gravel road in the direction of the Potosi Campground. The road twisted through a shallow canyon among hills covered with huge bushes of sagebrush and juniper. Clouds of dust from occasional oncoming vehicles gilded the air ahead. After driving for a few miles, Willy stopped his old Ford at the campground. We walked along the foot of a wooded mountain.

In the second half of the 19th century, prospectors mined here for gold. They had dug a hole at the exit of the hot spring next to the cold creek and outlined its edges with stones. They used to bathe their tired bodies in these mixed waters here after hard work. So did we. As if advised by Little Humpbacked

Horse from a Russian fairytale, we went down the stony steps into the cold creek, carefully approached the exit of boiling underground waters and sank our feet into the purest sand. The hot stream pleasantly tickled our heels. Blue-gray dragonflies hovered above the water, and only our bespectacled heads were seen above the surface. The eyeglasses fogged up quickly, but I had time to spot a couple of moose a hundred yards downstream. They grazed in the reeds and did not pay us any heed.

Mellow, Willy told me the story of his passion for bees:

"Before the collapse of the USSR, I caught tuberculosis and decided to move to the countryside for a while, to be closer to nature. I believed then and I still believe now that outdoor physical labor not only enriches, but also heals. I made a deal with a beekeeper and lived at his homestead for a whole summer. He taught me that without stimulative feeding, there won't be any good honey flow. A beekeeper must be as busy as a bee! But he did not allow me to care for the bees on my own. I cleaned the beehives and beehive frames, and melted the empty combs into beeswax. In short, I got an understanding of how to run an apiary. Ever since then, I've wanted to keep bees, but only here it became possible."

"And this does not interfere with your job, or your freedom of travel, or life in general?" I stopped talking, feeling for a cold stream with my right foot.

Willy looked at me with understanding, then threw his head back to look at the sky and said seriously, "Nah, Bro, it's actually the other way around. It helps to live conscientiously: you can't fool the bees."

Dizzy, we climbed out onto the rocks, feeling completely mellow. We threw our towels over our shoulders and ambled to the parking lot, which was a full mile away.

My friend was restless, and the next day we drove to some other places associated with the Gold Rush in the Wild West, like ghost towns of Virginia City and Bannack.

It was noon. The L-shaped gallows pole rose on the edge of Bannack.

"A sad exhibit," Willy said ironically.

Feeling a knot in my stomach, I noted, "Like on the edge of a cliff."

A tour guide came up, a young woman in a wide-brimmed hat. She told us the story of Henry Plummer, the Sheriff of Bannack, who was accused of having connections with the outlaw gang of the Innocents; he was hanged here in 1864.

"Those were wild times," said Willy, wiping large drops of sweat from his forehead.

"Nobody now can know what really happened," I added.

We stood on a hillock under the glaring sun. The prairie stretched far and wide, and only on the horizon mountains rose in a purple haze. A prairie dog popped out from its burrow, turned its head in our direction and froze.

"Can we go now?" I asked. "I don't like ghosts..."

"We still definitely need to go into the canyon and shoot at targets," Willy said when we returned home feeling completely exhausted, "I have a Mosin-Nagant rifle downstairs in the basement."

Soon it was time for me to return home: my business trip was over. I thanked Willy for his hospitality and took a flight to the East Coast, promising to come back.

In the winter, I received a strange letter from my friend:

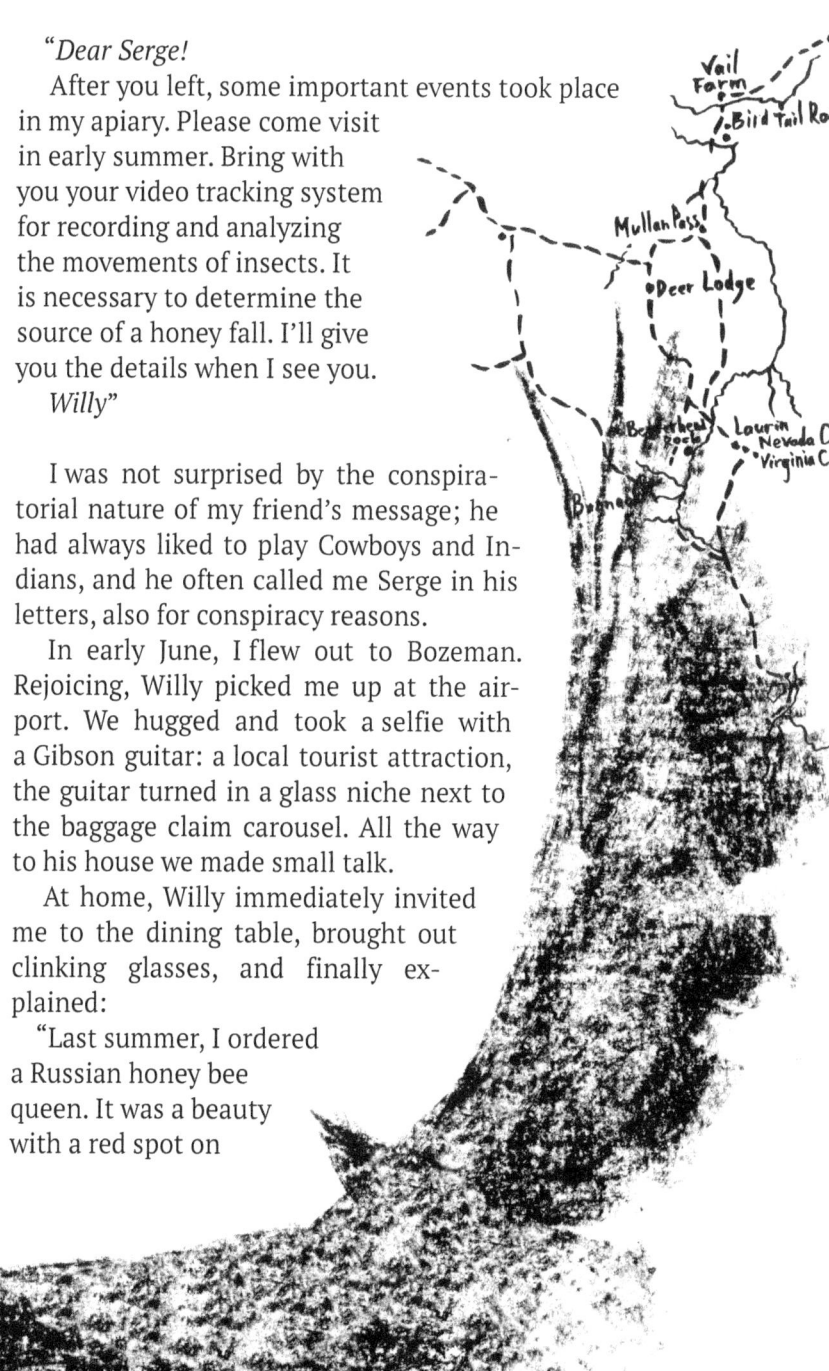

"Dear Serge!

After you left, some important events took place in my apiary. Please come visit in early summer. Bring with you your video tracking system for recording and analyzing the movements of insects. It is necessary to determine the source of a honey fall. I'll give you the details when I see you.

Willy"

I was not surprised by the conspiratorial nature of my friend's message; he had always liked to play Cowboys and Indians, and he often called me Serge in his letters, also for conspiracy reasons.

In early June, I flew out to Bozeman. Rejoicing, Willy picked me up at the airport. We hugged and took a selfie with a Gibson guitar: a local tourist attraction, the guitar turned in a glass niche next to the baggage claim carousel. All the way to his house we made small talk.

At home, Willy immediately invited me to the dining table, brought out clinking glasses, and finally explained:

"Last summer, I ordered a Russian honey bee queen. It was a beauty with a red spot on her thorax. I installed a nucleus box with the new queen bee at my neighbor's place. In August, when I was extracting the honey, I found a frame with unusual dark green honey in the hive with the Russian queen bee. Honey fall from juniper!"

Willy described in detail how this type of honey was generated: when there was a sharp drop in temperature, the juniper released sap; aphids fed on this sap and excreted undigested sugars in the form of drops that fell under the tree. Bees collected this honeydew or "honey fall" and processed it into pine honey.

"This kind of honey can be harmful to bees during the winter," Willy continued, pouring a golden drink from a plastic bottle, "but I didn't worry, because there was regular honey in other hives and it was still more than a month before the end of the honey harvest."

"Well, why look for the source of the pine honey then?" I was a little annoyed by the long preamble.

"In October, I was preparing for overwintering and moved bees from the nucleus box to a regular beehive," Willy continued, unperturbed. "I noticed strange particles on the bottom of the empty hive, they looked like bee-bread at first glance. They were like small yellow grains of sand. I collected them with some difficulty and analyzed them under a microscope: they turned out to be gold! I inspected other beehives: there were no such particles anywhere else!"

"Do you think that the presence of pine honey and gold dust in the same beehive is somehow connected?" I had an "Aha!" moment, finally.

"Exactly!" Willy exclaimed. "Either gold dust spilled on the honey fall, or vice versa, honey fall drops fell on a treasure of gold dust. When bees collected the honeydew, the smallest particles got stuck to their paws," and he put his legs up on a chair next to him.

"Hmm! "The Gold Fall"[49] is a fitting title for an adventure story," I chuckled. "Wait a minute! As a matter of fact, there is

---

[49] A novel written in 1945 by Nikolay S. Ustinovich, a Soviet writer.

such a piece of writing. I remember reading it. In my early days, I used to read all sorts of things."

"And for us it will be the name of a do-it-yourself project with a prize at the end," Willy returned to the table and poured the sparkling liquid into the glasses.

"By the way, why do you think this is a buried treasure?"

"Man!" Willy raised his hands. "Do you forget our trip a year ago?" He crossed the room to the window, then returned. "Gold was mined in this area from the middle of the 19th century until the Great Depression. Perhaps it was lost under some tragic circumstances."

"Is there a jewelry shop nearby?" I remembered "The Golden Rose"[50] by Konstantin Paustovsky. "Maybe some young lover collected precious dust. Aren't you afraid to get into a delicate situation?"

"There are only farms and ranches around," Willy retorted.

"So you say, we will go on a treasure hunt near the place where the beehive with the Russian queen bee sits?" I cautiously reached for tinned sardines. The tin container was carelessly opened with a knife, and the sharp bent edges stuck out.

"It's not that simple," Willy sighed. "Bees travel within a radius of about three miles. It is not that easy to find spilled gold dust in such an area. We need to track them somehow. I hope you remembered to bring your equipment."

I confirmed that the instruments were in my bag together with the laptop. We grabbed a drink, and then one more, and soon we began to build castles in the air:

"In the future, humans will fly like fairies!"

"Not just fly but collect specks of gold dust! *Golden dust of knowledge*[51]!"

---

[50] In this work, Konstantin Paustovsky discussed the process of literary creation.

[51] A quote from the work *Tales of Power* by Carlos Castaneda, an American writer.

We discussed our futurological forecasts a little. Suddenly, Willy exclaimed:

"But let's not wait for our wings to grow! We will get straight to business tomorrow morning!"

As long as I had known Willy, he was always stubborn, especially after drinking the iconic Buratino Lemonade,[52] a symbol of the long-gone Soviet times.

We spent the next two days adapting my equipment to treasure hunting. I must say a few words about it separately, especially since this device is no longer a secret.

About fifteen years ago, I had put together a device for studying the habits of laboratory mice. Later, I refined the equipment at home. I used my kitchen as a testing ground and cockroaches as test subjects. The software analyzed merged images from several video recorders and calculated parameters of insect movement. The device was useful for tracking small animals not only in a vivarium, but also in the field. Shortly after my first publications, I received a job offer from a university in the USA.

Last year, the nucleus box of bees sat on an island. This was completely wild private land. The island was about three miles long, and no more than half a mile wide.

The entire island was covered with abundant vegetation: grass was as tall as a man, junipers grew on the hillocks, and there were poplars, aspens, and thickets of blackberries and golden currant closer to the shore. The island had only three owners over the past one hundred years. Harry Legrand, its current owner, allowed us to continue the experiments with bees on his land although he warned us that it was a habitat for moose, and moose encounters could be dangerous.

Harry gave us the code to the ranch gate and left for a week on his business out of state. When he learned of the ultimate goal of our experiments, he assured us that he was not interested in gold; however, he entertained the possibility that it

---

[52] The lemonade is now readily available at some Russian-American grocery stores in the USA.

could make for an amusing tale. Before leaving, the rancher invited us to his house, and proudly showed us his collection of over fifty different types of barbed wire, some dating back to the American Civil War. I promised to enhance his collection and bring specimens of barbed wire from the ruins of the GULAG camps and transit points, as soon as the borders would be opened. The conversation drifted to the history of Montana. Harry sincerely believed in the guilt of Henry Plummer, the Sheriff of Bannack.

"When I was in college," he leaned closer, "I was already interested in this issue. The archives of the State of Montana kept the memoirs of a young lawyer, and I read them, and I learned that the mining area became safe after Plummer was hanged. And the lawyer wrote that it was said that *a man might lay a sack of gold dust down on the sidewalk and it would be there till the buckskin rotted off, before anyone touched it!*"[53] He sat back, tossing his curly hair.

Willy and I shrugged in disbelief.

The next day, we bought a scythe at Walmart and started on our project. We would have presented a very unusual picture if anyone had been there to see us: two men carrying a beehive and a scythe on a stretcher. I also had a messenger bag with a laptop, a set of video recorders, and several tripods. Willy brought a fishing trap basket along.

We crossed the creek over a dilapidated bridge. A few yards away, we trimmed some grass and set up the beehive. Willy opened the entrance block to the beehive, and several impatient bees immediately flew out. While I was affixing assorted devices to the tripods and arranging them, Willy ran over to the stream and threw the fishing trap into the water, first tying it with a long rope to a rock. Returning, he explained:

"I saw a tackle like that at the local museum. The Indians from an indigenous tribe used it for fishing. I've made a replica in my spare time; I have a passion for Indian accessories and

---

[53] Amede Bessette, "The Last Bandit Hanged in Bannack by the Vigilantes", Montana Historical Archives.

outfits. As a child, I read Fenimore Cooper novels, made Indian costumes from pigeon feathers, and we ran around the yard with my friends, wearing them. When I moved here, I realized that it was inappropriate to wear such costumes. What can I say, nowadays school kids have not even heard of Fenimore Cooper!" Willy gave a hopeless wave of his hand.

For the purposes of our "The Gold Fall" project, we equipped the hive entrance with about a dozen capacitive sensors, which were used in metal detectors. When a bee carrying gold dust came close to a sensor, a signal appeared in the electrical circuit, the flight path recorded a minute earlier was analyzed, and the computer generated data about the direction the insect flew in from.

The first day of observations did not bring any results. We had to prepare for a long watch, so we went to get food and sleeping bags.

I slipped into my sleeping bag and immediately fell asleep. In the morning, I had a dream. The two of us were in a narrow gorge; a stream gurgled somewhere in its depths. Willy attached a target to an old tree, just below a hollow. I peeked into the hollow: it reeked of cold and emptiness. Then I took a rifle, put the butt to my shoulder, aimed just below the bull's eye and fired. A swarm of bees burst from the hollow and quickly flew in our direction. The bees surrounded me; they got into my mouth and ears and stung me furiously. In pain and fear, I threw the rifle down, ran, then fell; hugging the ground, I rolled into the canyon, which turned into a huge hollow expanding in all directions... I woke up.

Late in the afternoon the installation triggered the first alarm.

"It worked, it worked!" I shouted.

Yet the route of the precious bees was far from being accurately recorded. As a rule, when a bee approaches a hive, it flies in a spiral. To ascertain the exact direction, we needed to collect a certain number of "positive events".

How long did we have to wait? Who knew... The evening was getting chilly, but we didn't want to get out of the wilderness, and I didn't want to leave the equipment unattended. We built a hut, sort of like an Indian teepee: we cut down several thin aspens, tied their tops together, and wrapped them with an old tent flap. We gathered twigs from the nearest brushwood and lit a campfire. Willy dragged over a half-rotten log with beaver teeth marks on the end of the trunk. Giving thanks to the beaver, we sat down on the log.

It was getting dark when a moose approached the campsite. Captivated by strange smells, it stood for several minutes, then pensively turned towards the stream to drink. I breathed a sigh of relief: all this time I had worried about the safety of the instruments.

As soon as the moose was gone, Willy remembered the fishing trap. Using his flashlight, he ran to the stream, and pulled the trap out by the rope. There were only fingerling fish inside. Willy wanted to release them, but I stopped him: a recipe of my mother's came to mind. I arranged the small fish in an even layer in a frying pan, covered them with eggs, and fried them.

"My mother did this when she lived in the resettlement community called "Beacon of Communism". Just before her death, she told me about her childhood, how her mother and grandparents were resettled from Opochka to Siberia."

"Dekulakization?" Willy asked and threw a dry twig into the fire. The twig immediately caught.

"Dekulakization[54] began later. This resettlement was initiated by the famine of the 1920s, after the Civil War. Unfortunately, the complete history of those events has not yet been written."

The twigs were crackling peacefully in the fire; we watched the flames in silence. I found it hard to believe that we had a motor vehicle parked only a hundred yards away.

After a while, Willy engaged me in a heart-to-heart conversation. And it didn't matter that we were far away from our homeland. Willy recalled his first winter here, and how stunned he was by the vastness of the prairie and the mountains around. Once he put his skis on right next to his house and skied to the nearest canyon, crossing through the snow-

---

[54] *Dekulakization* was a Soviet campaign of political repression, including arrests, deportation, or execution of millions of *kulaks* (prosperous peasants) and their families.

---

covered fields: it never occurred to him that they were all privately owned. That time he got away with it; no one seemed to mind.

Every three hours, I monitored the computer to see whether "positive events" accumulated. Three days later we were able to calculate the azimuth. The direction was north-north-east.

"The unknown path is ours. We nailed it!" Willy brightened up and put a shovel over his shoulder.

"Let's see what an independent experiment demonstrates," I muttered indistinctly and dubiously and equipped myself with a metal detector.

We followed the compass precisely and observed each bush on the way, checking whether there was any honey fall. Finally, fifty yards before the northernmost point of the island, we reached a small area of higher ground with scattered juniper trees. Their old branches were covered with aphids; sweet honey fall drops fell onto the ground, and ants and some wild wasps were busily crawling in it.

Using the metal detector, we searched every square yard beneath the trees. Under a tree on the eastern side, next to a broken branch, we found an oval pendant with a scarab on it. Quite probably its chain had been caught by the branch, and the pendant hung for a long time on this century-old juniper tree, until it fell to the ground. I picked it up by the chain. At that moment, the setting sun was still illuminating the spot we were at, and the bug sparkled in the last rays. The pendant was ajar, and traces of dark gold dust could be seen on the inner surface of its flaps.

"Looks like fine-dispersed gold," my friend suggested. "When sand is washed for gold, gold mud remains in the river, consisting of the smallest particles, which are in fact a very fine-dispersed gold dust. It is incredibly difficult, almost impossible, to extract it with the help of old-fashioned mining technologies."

On the spot where the pendant had lain, honeydew drops shone golden. I collected them in a plastic bag, but the metal detector continued to sound off alarms. Willy took a shovel and began digging diligently. Twilight was near when, after about a yard, the shovel hit something solid. We were overwhelmed with excitement. It was a small forged chest, and next to it a human skeleton stuck out of the ground. There was no lock on the chest. Willy pushed the lid open with the shovel. A musty smell wafted from the chest. We were extremely disappointed, as we found the chest almost empty: inside there was only a half-decayed shirt, a few coins, and a leather bound notebook with an aged brass clasp.

"Let Legrand deal with this box and the skeleton; let him invite the archaeologists." Willy flipped through the notebook, shook clay off his jeans and picked up our tools. "But the notebook can be a valuable find. Let's keep it."

Looking at this notebook, I suddenly realized that no one would ever be able to find a diary of my grandmother, or her parents: they had all been illiterate. I picked up the shovel. Stumbling, I followed Willy on our way back.

Although the notebook was handwritten in perfect cursive, we could hardly tell what was written there: so many lines were blurred by moisture. All evening Willy felt down and did not even hide his annoyance.

"Not much of a prize..."

I tried to cheer him up, but in doing so, I only increased his irritation. So, the next morning I decided to return home to the East Coast.

Two weeks later, I received a message from Willy:

"*Dear Serge!*

I gave the notebook we had found to a Professor in the History Department at the local University. He managed to read the diary entries. They shed light on the story of Henry Plummer, the Sheriff of Bannack. The notebook belonged to a friend of Plummer's. He had left Bannack and joined John Bozeman's group after Plummer's death sentence was carried out. According to the notebook entries, Plummer was innocent of the crimes he had been charged with. Can you imagine the expression on Legrand's face when he learned about this?!

But this is only part of the story. I managed to find a way to encourage bees to collect honeydew. I propose to use bees next year to search for gold dust along the Mullan Road that used to connect Fort Benton and Fort Hall: people transported gold here during the Gold Rush. What do you think?
Your friend,
Willy"

What to say to my persistent friend? I scanned the latest news: the People's Republic of Seattle had lasted three weeks and was overrun by the police the day before. The leader of the interim government had fled, dressed as a woman. Closing the laptop, I went to the window and pulled back the curtain. There was a crowd of Black Lives Matter protesters in the street. No one flipped cars over, or burglarized shops: today's protest was peaceful. A group of young people crowded around the Bishop's Inn.

I returned to the table. A jar of golden honey stood there, a gift from Willy. I brewed fireweed tea and took a sip. I tapped my fingers on the oak tabletop, thinking.

Bees, bees... And what do the bees have to do with this? Bee Lives Matter too. The ancient Egyptians allegedly thought, The tears of the God of Sun turn into bees. Hmm, curious.

I felt light-headed as if I had taken a swig of a stiff drink just a minute ago.

It means that if we follow the bees, we can find our way to the Sun, or rather, to our Maker!

Night was falling. I went to bed thinking: *Tomorrow I must research how to save the world.*